THE OLD ASIANS CLAP

THE OLD ASIANS CLAP

John Dempsey

Iriswhite Publishing
North Carolina

The Old Asians Clap

Iriswhite Publishing
North Carolina
For information, visit www.iriswhite.com

ISBN-10: 0-9711072-8-9
ISBN-13: 978-0971107281
Library of Congress Control Number: 2007939960
FIRST EDITION

Dedicated to livers, lungs, hearts and urinary tracts
the world over.
Dedicated to chewed fingernails, itchy nights,
rough mornings and lying mirrors
world-wide.

Dedicated to personal globes, homemade rockets,
and the little gods we all keep in our shirtfront
pockets.

Dedicated to all of you, and to all of me, and to the
little man on the inside who pushes all our buttons.
Dedicated to old milk.
Dedicated to pill connections.
Dedicated to sluggish blood, sour dreams, and all
the curses hurled at ceilings
when no one
upstairs
cares to listen.

TABLE OF CONTENTS

Dedication v

Table of Contents vii

Intro Story 3
A Pretty 8
An Audience Of One 9
An Easy Solution 11
An Egyptian Working His Way
   Towards The Asians 12
Autograph 12
Notes On A Bar Napkin 13
Changing And Staying The Same 13
I'll Meet You More Than Halfway 15
Fight At The Bank 15
I Could've Been 20
Commute- Conversation- (Plus My View
   From The Observatory!) Cut-up 21
Chicago – Part 1 22
Chicago – Part 2 24
Confession 29
I Wonder What She Called Me 33
Hot Tub Thoughts 34
Gotta Get Over 35
He Woke Up Thinking 36
The Regular Band 36
Making Deals With... 37
Manhattan Appreciation 38
On The Train Ride Home Last Night 39
Pointing Fingers In The Right Direction 40
Looking Around, Questioning 41
My Practical Feet 42
My Wed Morning Rant To Ric (My
   Hotel Reverie) 44

– Table of Contents –

Mamma-Mamma 45
The Italian's Got It Wrong (Or This
    Easy Weakness) 46
Postcard From The Bahamas 46
Seasons Greetings 46
Simple Swan Dives From High Cliffs 47
Problems And Dreams 48
Shadows Collide (Acoustic) 49
That Kid On Pulaski 50
Trumpet Solo For The Blues 52
I Could've Been 53
The Old Asians Clap 54
The Worst Is 54
The IQ Test – Pretension, Analysis,
    A Nice Little Story 55
Underbelly Of The Melting Pot 59
What Happens Is 60
Worse Than Poison Ivy 61
Untitled 61
I Could've Been 63
We Were Lying On The Beach 63
The Eel In A Hammock 68
We Were In A Car 69
Entrepreneurs 71
Redecoration, Confusion, The Great Pharaoh
    Dempsey On His Throne! 75
A Fan, A Few Emails, And Some Photos 82
The Big Top Orgy 84
The Quickie 85
Waiting On A Connection With
    The Music Lover 86
To Sit On A Beach In Mexico 90
The Rolling Circus And A Sweater 93

– Table of Contents –

A Not So Strong Constitution 104
The Eaters Of Chocolate 104
That's It. Sure. 113
Simple Things 114
Paranoid? 114
I Could've Been 118
Great Moments 119
Imagine That 119
West 3rd Symmetry 123
Correspondence (A Building Block) 124
Reflection 129
Exorcism 130
Friday Night With All That Speed 131
It Hides 135
In Preparation 136
She Looks At Me In The Hammock 136
Offering To The Gods 137
Who's In Charge? 138
Argument 138
Every Waking Second 139
Construction Problems 140
Goals 140
He Said 141
How I Lost My Copy 142
Great Expectations 145
Horticulture- Propagation 145
#3 146
I Could've Been 148
#4 148
How We All Became Killers 150
I Could've Been 156
Why Trains? 157
Roger 159

– Table of Contents –

*Self-Appraisal (In Answer To Good Old
    Mr. Henry, The Italian Poet)* 163
Self Assurance 164
Your Own 165
Understanding 166
Those 4 Horrible Women On The Train 168
Practice Makes Perfect 171
Computer Crashes When I'm Typing 172
Almost 173
#5 174
#6 176
Following In His Footsteps 177
The Compliment 177
Gambling 178
We Were Clams 178
The Tracks Were On Fire 179
I Bought It 180
My Dirty Muse 181
Metrosexuals! Manhattan! The 21st Century! ... 185
Movies? John? It Could Happen. 189
Movies? John? It Could Happen – Part 2 192
The Dempsey Institute Of Literature 193
I Could've Been 200

THE OLD ASIANS CLAP

☯ INTRO STORY

I sat down. The machine was powered up, and it was a good feeling, better than any of the feelings I'd had in months.

There was no question about it; this was gonna be a fantastic story, *Milk to the Cat*. Yes. It was about a 27 year old Ecuadorian girl who lived on a diet of semen and canned tuna fish. It would be filled with insight; it would be a cross-section of the female mentality, sure. I brought up a blank page, typed two sentences, and froze.

They were bad sentences. There wasn't any light in them. They were flat, one-dimensional strings of words. They were shit, and all my good feeling turned to milk left sitting in August sun.

I didn't have to wonder why. I had done it to myself, systematically screwing myself, step by step, over the past 2 years. The Struggle for Money! It started with the fishing journal; 1500 words a week for 200 dollars a month. Then the movie script; traveling to Boulder, Colorado to meet with the Director and the film editor, watching old films, curbing style in order to fit between the lines. And then the newspaper; assignments that had me researching, quoting, playing at journalist instead of at poet, fantastic, Johnny you've fucked yourself to pay bills, to feed your monkeys, to maintain a sedated, drunken, pupil-dilated lifestyle!

I didn't want it to happen, the despair.

"You're just trying to survive. There's no shame in that. Forget it. (It isn't easy. Sometimes, well, sometimes I'm under the impression I've got integrity.) But it's the past. Forget it! The past is dinosaurs in the tar. Is broken condoms and morning after pills. Is dead hair left in the teeth of a brush. (I know, I know.)

Just stay calm. (I'm trying.) Go for a walk. Smoke a cigarette. Maybe stop at The Red Lion and have a beer. (O.K.) Just do it. (I'll give it a shot.) Don't you know who you are? (Sometimes I wonder about that. Seriously.) You idiot! You're John Dempsey! One of the greatest writers of your generation! Maybe even of the 21st Century! (You really think so?) I know so. You're all of your heroes, but magnified, and rolled into a dynamic jumble of flesh and thought! (Maybe I am.) Yes! You are! You're kamikaze pilots at Pearl Harbor! (You're right!) You're the bullet that killed Kennedy! You are the will and jizz of the Ever-Fucking Cosmos!"

I made The Red Lion. There were 2 people in there; the bartender and an older guy sitting at the end of the bar. I sat opposite the older guy and told the bartender to start a tab.

"Budweiser. In the bottle."

When it came I drank it. The last sip told me it wasn't enough.

"Let me get another beer."

I noticed the older guy staring at me. I stared back, taking inventory. His lips were cracked and peeling. His eyebrows were white, long, sprouting from his face and hanging over his eyes. There was white stubble on his cheeks and neck. Spider veins on the nose. He looked chewed up and spit out by some machine greater than his personal I, the machine of Life and Time, the machine of the Sidewalk, the machine of the Bottle.

I kept staring, hoping that my I was made up of something stronger. He licked his lips, opened his mouth, a prelude to speech and I saw yellows, browns, the blacks of gaps.

"You too good to sit next to me?"

"I just like my personal space."

"Think you're better than me, don't you?"

"No, just hoping old man."

"Young prick. You're the same as everybody else. You see a guy down on his luck and you turn your nose up, like I'm garbage, like I'm dog shit."

"Look, I came in here to think, not talk to some old drunk."

"Too good to even talk to me, ha, young prick. Well it's your loss."

"I'm sure of it."

"I could help you, you know."

"I doubt that."

"Oh yeah? Well at least I know what's wrong with you."

He was staring at me, hard, and smiling, like my skin was transparent and he saw right into me. I looked down at my hand; skin, bones, some hair, fingernails, wart on the index finger, but nothing you could see through.

"Alright, you tell me what's wrong with me and I'll buy your next drink."

"Bartender! I'll take a double Glen Livet."

"Hey! After you tell me."

"What's your name?"

"John."

"Well John…"

"Yeah?"

"You're a pile of shit-filled intestines attached to an uncooperative asshole."

The bartender looked at me. I sat stunned for a second before nodding my head.

I walked over to the stool next to him and sat down.

"What happened to your personal space?"

"How'd you know I was blocked?"

"I could just tell."

I looked at my hand again. I still couldn't see through it.

"Don't worry, it's not that you're easy to read, it's just that this is where we happen to be."

"What do you mean?"

He looked down at his glass, he looked at the bottles behind the bar, then drained the Glen Livet.

"Bartender. Another round."

We waited for the drinks. He didn't move, twitch, nothing. A statue. I couldn't tell if he was breathing. I got nervous. This drunk knew something and I wanted to know that something too. I was about to check for a pulse when the drinks came.

Reanimation! He turned on his stool and pointed out the window.

"This is New York City. Almost everybody around here is an artist. At least in their heads. All you've got to do is look at them; if they're smiling, then they're producing, if they look constipated, like you did when you walked in, well, then they're in limbo, trapped between the thought and the action."

He drained the Glen Livet.

"But what can I do to get out of that limbo, how do I fix myself?"

He continued staring out the window. He was playing with me, and I knew it. And I didn't like it. I've always been an impatient person. When I was 4 years old I got sick and drank a bottle of prescription cough syrup. I stumbled around my parent's house, falling into the walls and giggling. When my mother asked me why I did it I said, "Feel better fast."

I worked to stay calm. My first impulse was to crack my bottle against the bar, threaten him with it, force him to cough up the answers I was looking for. I checked it.

"Bartender!"

The drinks were put down in front of us. He turned away from the window and reached for his drink. I beat him to it. I moved the glass out of his reach, and just sat there, working on my beer and staring off into space. He looked at me. Once he realized I wasn't budging it came out.

"From what I can tell, you're scared. It's no good. Drop that fear and everything will open up."

"But exactly what is it that I'm scared of?"

"Everything! You're a coward. Just look at yourself. Right now you're scared that I won't help you out of your hole, but what you don't realize is that you don't need help, just a kick in the ass."

I passed him the drink. He one-sipped it. I sat there, thinking about what he had said. He was right. I am a coward. I have a thousand irrational fears: ticks, dentists, zombies, others- I'm scared of ringing telephones, white cats, pesto sauce. But it was more than that. My fears, my real fears; the deep rooted terrors that force my soul to quiver and shit itself, they were made up of something different. Something unknown.

"You know what makes astronauts so great?"

"What's that?"

"They have no fear of the unknown. They get blasted off of mother earth and go rushing towards the darkness of space. There could be a million deaths waiting for them just past the stratosphere, yet they strap themselves in, all systems go! Blast off! And they go rumbling and shooting off into the heavens. They make attempts at the unknown."

"Yeah, those astronauts sure are great people."

The old drunk then turned at me with more speed and life than I thought him capable of. He grabbed me by the shirt and shook me around in my stool. I was holding a beer bottle and it slipped out of my hand, fell through space, and shattered on the floor. The bartender started walking over.

"Hey, none of that shit in here!"

The old drunk was still holding me by the shirt. I was frozen. His eyes bulged out of their sockets. His hands shook with rage. Then he opened his mouth and I felt the heat of a thousand fiery female crotches exploding against my face.

"Don't be an idiot! Be an astronaut! You must make attempts at the unknown!"

"What do you mean?"

"You two better cut it out!"

"You know what I mean!"

"But I'm not sure that I do."

"I said cut it out!"

"Go! Right now! You know! Blast off, you jackass!"

And he let go of my shirt. And I jumped out of my stool, ran for the door. Behind me I heard the bartender yelling.

"Hey, you didn't pay for..."

I was already gone, running fast, my feet hit the pavement same as my fingers were hitting a keyboard and I kept going, faster and harder, dropping fears, worries, uncertainties, forgetting cares, blasting off, the stratosphere! Yes! And soon I was back in front of the machine, the words were all there, just waiting for me. I was back at it,

making attempts

at the unknown.

Ꮼ A PRETTY

maybe you stand lean, tall, the sun cutting in sharp all around
you,
a playful hand
hovering...
holstered at the hip
a Western silhouette, playing a pretty
dangerous
young man or
maybe you're a mix:
one part desperate
and one part determined,
awake for two days, driving from Queens to New Orleans
to bury
your dead love, or maybe
you're like me; just some kid in a small room,

typing movie scripts, short stories, poems, sure, the cosmos
unfolding behind your eyes, snorting Aderol, looking in the
mirror

and smiling
at the reflection of a pretty
dangerous

young man

෬ AN AUDIENCE OF ONE

your poems aren't read
your books don't sell
nobody laughs at the lines in your stories
as loud
as you do when you're typing.

it doesn't matter. it shouldn't bother you.

the only time
you should worry

is when you stop…when pens run dry, when pages stay blank,
when there's no humor in your reflection…that's when you can
start to worry. but for now

while the keyboard is singing…ah, it's better than being a
cashier in a supermarket,

isn't it john? of course.

and better than selling oranges or roses along the highway. yes.
better than mopping floors and scrubbing toilets. much better. it
beats frying burgers for chubby kids in some fast food place
when schools let out.

it beats raking leaves off of lawns.
it beats washing dishes.
it beats masturbating to memories with a rubber hose wound
around your throat. I agree.

so john?

yeah?

no more tears?

not a drop.

think of all the other traps you could've fallen into.

I know.

think of all the narrow escapes, think of all the negative test
results, all the luck
you've had so far.

I know.

remember that an audience of one can still bring down a house,
given that the house
is small enough,
and that one
claps hard enough.

an audience of one?

that's right, an audience of one, your biggest fan, and guess
what?

what?

who's your biggest fan, huh Johnny boy? well,

I guess I am!

that's right, and who's your toughest critic?

I am!

and who do you have to please?

no one except myself!

ah, you're learning John, little

by little...and so

while others count out change, sell oranges, scrub, fry, rake,
wash, jack-off into photo albums,
while bulls rush young Spaniards,

while women bleed for 7 days,
while dogs howl at earthquakes in China…there's a CLAP,
CLAP, CLAP, while an audience
of one
works on bringing down
the house.

℞ AN EASY SOLUTION

i just drive to vermont and lose it, wonder what's happening in
new york, but

don't

really care i'm

no more than a regular kid (just smoking dope and snow-
boarding the un-

occasional bottle (dewars) just)

looking

for an escape in mountains different from architecture different
from metro card having to swipe at the right angle with the right
speed to get you through the turnstile before something behind
you gets upset with more mole on her face than unfulfilled

egg

in her gut and time, always time, waiting on the C, on the A
reading some

one better

than yourself…you eventually say 'Fuck It' (once again, The
Scribe) you say fuck it and 7-11 three miles from the mountain's
got a liquor section enough to turn a stable on its back and
looking rigid, you just drive somewhere different from…

and…

lose it

‌❦ AN EGYPTIAN WORKING HIS WAY
TOWARDS THE ASIANS...

The farthest
you'll ever get
is trying to understand it

not solving, don't even think about it, it's beyond you, there isn't
a question; you're only given enough brains and enough

curiosity to ask, but try figuring out, understanding it...

then walk 20 years around a joke with the most depressing (yet,
goddamned liberating 'Whatever I do is meant to be done in just
that way.') punch line there ever was. "Consciousness" he says,
"it's gotta be the worst

banana peel slip
of all time."

❦ AUTOGRAPH

are you kidding me I'll
never stock shelves, create lines, re-write scripts for Paramount
or

Universal, hell, Barnes &

Noble's out of the question (corporeally speaking) yet Iriswhite

for some reason

actually

accepts me...in print,

I'm better than roger moore in the saint, better than disturbed
cobwebs in cunts after 10 years of shower heads and handyman

commercials...sure, just put it down in ink and I'll

sign my name to it

෨ NOTES ON A BAR NAPKIN

2:30 am red spot on my collar bone, back me on this next shot and

I'll make certain phone calls.

understand cryptography? psychology of chemicals? the importance of first impressions and root matters? most important step in crossing un-crossable distance is strong bass line like backbone and a certain confidence…I've been playing at polo shirt,

sharp creased, neck
tied, red drops on my collar bone and I assume it's the inevitability of decay-
the nose-

I shouldn't of made certain phone calls, but (john and all that I am) 'I've
got all the right numbers, memorized…' bleeding
14 hour martyr, caught in the

Chinese finger cuff of science (the help/hurt, screwed if you do if you don't), detention center of a planet…'Doc, if I had enough drive,

I'd break through the wall of vaccine, (adaptable virus with evolution on the mind (john that I am)), I'd

infect bodies.'

෨ CHANGING AND STAYING THE SAME

They used to turn out men made of stone like *break the mold the globe just can't handle too many of these guys*- there wasn't any going to sleep, there weren't any closed eyes, there were a lot more people yelling, laughing, screwing and wrestling, all night 3, 4, 5, 6 am, no questions asked and I now sit around here, looking at the closed eyes, being kissed goodnight and taking out an air mattress, I've got to retire, and keep all this energy to myself.

What is it? Aderol. So now I found something new, perfect, exactly what I needed, something that gives me my coke head without the itchy rotten guilty morning come-down, something I snort 40 milligrams of sweet as sugar apple candy pie and watch all these people sleep, hear them snore, plus they drool and I'm awake, tweaked all fucken out, and jumpy, scratchy, type, type, typity on the keyboard- things that can't be helped.

Just sitting here (outside of myself) and dealing with sleeping beautiful woman, beautifully Lisa, my beautiful love my muse breathes so heavy when she's in bed. My gas pump, my lifeblood, the only one that ever had such an effect on… this is what winds up happening. Always.

I wind up being the kid that can't sleep closing in on sunrise, closing in on 28 years old and twice the intake of any other engine on the line, twice the balls, twice the gamble, twice the problem as most anyone else; I push these internal limits, I force my self to push and move beyond my self, just keep going don't stop-

reminds of when I was typing *steps to the madhouse* and I couldn't be touched by time, traffic lights, policemen or dead batteries, nothing, not a mouse not a soul not even a pair of middle-aged legs with wet office gray cubical dreams of squiring a young fuck-up on her mind could touch me…

but she would send me t-shirts, and a flask, also demerol, and vicodin once, oh S. you helped out a whole lot when I was looking for most anything to bloom in bright orange…and now sitting here, still, with two beers for both hands like the great

dissolving artist

I've always been, I

disappear.

○R I'll Meet You More Than Halfway

even if I lose 19 times out of 20
if I drink every night of the calendar
and wake up here and there with a memory if

I type a thousand empty pages
and wind up
with
3

lines of (real, actual, something beyond my heroes, beyond my
dreams, my self, something beyond my screaming and scratching
at the walls, just 3 good lines that make you feel and stop and
stop reading for just a second...oh

muse or whatever you are just give me a few lines of) poetry

I think it'll be worth it

○R Fight At The Bank

It came to $350 for 40 vicodin and a half-ounce of mid-grade
green- expensive.

But this is New York; police state that it is, flophouse that it is,
flickering light bulb of a state with the power to attract single-
minded (I want to say, self-destructive, yet, it's in a
subconscious way, it's a deep and rooted glitch of the back brain,
the seed planted during the embryo stage, an innate bend...)
flickering light bulb of a state that it is, swinging on a back
porch, attracts single-minded moths- 350! New York-

Where a man's standard of living decreases in direct relation,
I'd say a 1 to 1 ratio, to the thinnest hand on his wristwatch.
Where you can see (without squinting, peering over a fence, or
even having to buy a ticket) the cost of comfortable, chemical
lifestyle swell up to so many grams per dollar, so many shots in a
bottle, only so many nights to a paycheck... New York!

The vicodin ran 5.50 a pop but supposedly it was worth it; big, pink capsules, hundreds heaped upon hundreds of milligrams, enough to get your pupils dilated, enough to make you sit back, stare off into space... comfortable, chemical lifestyle.

We pulled up to the ATM (I was with The Blonde, the infamous, 3 feet of chain-smoking long hair) one of those drive up tellers, March 2nd, bank accounts like full gas tanks, the both of us, and she took out $180, no problem.

I saw an old model Jeep Wrangler pull up behind us, painted grey, pop music spilling out of the window, runs down the side of the car and floods the parking lot- a large puddle of nauseating sound, 92 cents below the lowest octave of E-flat... I gave The Blonde my bankcard and told her my pin number.

She fumbles with the card- between lit cigarette, incessant motion of hairbrush, adjustment of volume, counting of cash and answering of cell phone- it isn't surprising. The card drops and she has to open the car door, lean out, stretch...the retrieval, "What's your pin number again?" I tell her.

"Checking or Savings?"

"Checking."

"How much should I take out?"

"200." (Bank accounts like full gas tanks! The both of us! Vicodin!)

"What the hell is taking so long?" She asks while the ATM machine whirrs, buzzes, clicks in its native tongue: modulate-demodulate...

"I don't know."

Behind us the grey Jeep Wrangler, guy's lowered his radio in order to start honking. It's only been 5 minutes.

"What's that guy honking at?" I ask. Meanwhile, Blonde's got her head out the window, turns to the Wrangler.

"Just a second buddy." Then turns back to the machine, "Shit." she says, the whirrs, clicks and all have stopped, and across the screen: You have reached your maximum withdrawal limit for today. We are sorry for the inconvenience.

Behind us the grey Jeep Wrangler, guy's stopped honking in order to start yelling.

"C'mon damnit! Let's fucking go already!"

"Relax asshole, can't you see we're trying to get money?" Blonde's got no tolerance for the rudeness of strangers. I'm quiet about the whole thing. Mind occupied: Maximum withdrawal limit? Inconvenience? What do you mean?

I tallied up all the purchases I had made since my check cleared: 1 tin of Drum tobacco, an extra pack of rolling papers and 300 Top filter tips, a large bag of Gummy Rattlesnakes, 2 sticks of peppered beef jerky, a box of Japanese condoms, a 9-ft steel rail with a kink in the middle that I planned on using in the snowboard park I've been building in my parent's driveway, 1 case- Bud cans, an order of buffalo wings, 30 dollars for gas, paid insurance, credit card bills and car loan…but still, March 2nd, I should have close to 1,800 bucks, plus my line of credit and 8 o'clock meeting with this pill kid 10 minutes from now- Shit!

I get out of my head and rejoin the scene in the parking lot. Blonde's in a full-blown screaming match, guy in the Wrangler's foaming at the mouth, they're going back and forth, cursing, insulting one another, middle finger and the guy in the Wrangler makes a mistake.

"Fuck you, you stupid cunt!"

"Did he just call me a cunt? John? … John?"

I'm already out of the car (Maximum withdrawal limit?), fast as all hell (10 minutes from now, three hundred and fifty bucks, all those milligrams; pink, ready, waiting for me to come along with my strong teeth, with my single-minded moth self, with my deeply rooted glitches, my natural bend, my instinctive reaction and who's this guy think he is calling her…) I start moving towards the jeep…New York!

(A tangent!

New York breeds all types, all kinds, every variety and species of man you can think of. From muscle-bound street fighters that carry screwdrivers in their glove compartments, to the closed/locked closet door debutantes, pirouetting in sister's high heels, trying to look past chin stubble and Adam's apples- New York!

More than a melting pot, more than a point of intersection on a map, not just a place where different cultures, foreign races, strange colors, alien eyes, teeth and bone structure collide, not just an integrated society made up of ship jumping immigrants from all parts of the globe, more than a meeting ground for extraterrestrials with slanted eyes- New York!

A pool of primordially insane jism and egg; the recipe calling for the semen milked from a thousand deranged and ancient pricks mixed with the ova spilled out of a thousand imbalanced snatches- New York!

The breeding area for everything from pill popping young screw-ups that write under a name like John Dempsey to loudmouthed, nutless and gutless wonders who are blessed with grey Jeep Wranglers, fine vocal cords and a wide ranging, gutter-mouth vocabulary but not a Cervical, Dorsal, Thoracic or Lumbar vertebrae in sight when they get under the x-ray machine of a street lamp (my instinctive reaction and who's this guy think he is calling her a...).)

I'm moving, carrying myself forward, into the situation, my instinctive reactions, my New York upbringing...I take note that there's a girl in the passenger seat- that's good, better than it being one of his buddies- and she looks harmless, a bit chubby, wearing glasses.

The guy doing all the honking, cursing and cunt calling, the driver of the Wrangler, the loudmouthed, nutless wonder, all of a sudden, (it's the way I approach the car that does it; calculating, steady, my eyes fixed, it's the lethal determination of my movements, like, like rockslide, avalanche, like flash flood, like auto that's been parked on a steep hill and the E-brake gives out...I'm the cycle of a perfectly balanced wheel spinning off into eternity. I'm the inevitability of Newton's gravity. I'm a process that once set into motion cannot be stopped until some pre-programmed goal has been accomplished) like, like sugar cubes in hot water…

all of a sudden guy crumbles in his car seat and turns whitefish pale. I see him jerking at the stick shift and hear grinding gears. Guy can't move forward without slamming into The Blonde's car, and he just can't seem to get it into reverse, the whitefish gone even whiter, a bone soaked in Clorox then left out in the sun, he sticks his head through the open window, March 2nd at 8 pm, 26 degrees and the sweat ((regardless of the weather) who'd this guy think he was dealing with…) stands out fresh in big drops along his forehead.

"What're you gonna do? Hit my car?" In a new voice, he had picked up a quiver while trying to get into gear. And of course, me,

"No, I'm going to knock your fucking teeth out," real calm, too, like I'm talking about the weather, fishing tackle, the shape of a cloud…my deliberate motions, my deliberate intonation, a slow moving landslide, the sluggish avalanche (from street fighters to cross dressers, from Johns to jellyfish…it breeds all types).

I reach in the driver's side window as the Jeep's bucking back and forth, grinding gears, sweating fish, bunch up the guy's shirt in my left hand while cocking back with the right, planning to put my shoulders and back into the swing…Dempsey vs. Sharkey- 1927! I can hear The Blonde in the stands; laughing her ass off,

"No one calls me a cunt and gets away with it!" She loves it. I'm the white knight (sure!) defending her honor.

Nutless, gutless, spineless, loudmouthed driver finally gets the car into reverse. He punches the gas and I'm forced to pull my arm back out of the window. Then he finds first gear. Comes at me, fast. I jump out of the way, last second, would've clipped my thigh if I hadn't.

He pulls out of the parking lot and stops the car. I start moving towards him again. The whitefish, finding a hole in the net, spitting out the hook, slipping off the gaffe, back in the safety of the ocean so to speak, regains those fine vocal cords...

"You think you're tough? You're nothing but white trash! And your bitch is ugly too!"

I'm no longer the deliberate, slow moving landslide. I pick up speed. No longer the sluggish avalanche. No longer walking. I've become full blown raging river, white water rapids and all, running at the Jeep, fast as my legs can carry me, twice the amount of lethal determination as before...I'd be scared of myself in that situation.

Whitefish gets the picture, a squeal of tires, guy peals out onto the main road, a strong scent of Summer's Eve in his wake.

Blonde pulls up alongside of me, money in hand- turns out I was overdrawn on my checking account, savings, on the other hand ...- and I hop in the passenger seat.

"Follow that fucking Jeep Kitty Kat! He's not getting away with this!"

In The Blonde's Mitsubishi, "I love you John." 60 miles an hour down badly lit roads, "You're absolutely-" tight turns and he's got a lead on us, quarter past 8 with enough money for a binge "-fucking crazy." and the pill kid waiting for us...

5 minutes later without a blink of tail or brake light of hope (our comfortable, chemical lifestyle) we said screw it.

↭ I COULD'VE BEEN

the world's greatest lover

with the fingers of a pianist

a tongue like running horses and the cock

of a Frenchman

ೞ Commute- Conversation- (plus my view from the observatory!) Cut-up

adidas
crotch-less
checkered
gold
buckle

please do not
hold fireflies
in the garden, stand clear
next stop

thong, thong, grandma, big ass, too big, thong, staircase,
sunshine, street wet,

garbage
truck reek, old pigeon
cold corner
shivering, shitting, legs

tired, wings
in need
of repair, those aged
aviator
eyes- no shine- curbside, newspapers, worn shoes, worn face,
worn out, worn down

man,
paper cup, urine
streaked
yellow
teeth and
spare
change,

out of your mind, no bra, just right

even the old
pigeon lets

out a
grey
coo
before
toppling over, breeze from the east, pigeon soul like a kite,

phantom
paparazzi
click- click- clicking from 'What I'd call an obscene vantage
point.

Corner the whole fucken market
with their
ungodly
procedures!'

ℭℛ CHICAGO – PART 1

Now they were sitting on the couch. He had started out with
strips of bark, twigs, and crumpled up balls of newspaper. He
then added small branches, one by one and at cross angles, until
they caught. Eventually he put 2 big logs in the fire. They were
staring at the fire. He sat at the end of the couch with a pillow on
his lap. She had her head on the pillow.

"Chicago?" she asked.

"Yes?"

"What are you thinking about?"

"Nothing much, just looking at the fire."

He was thinking that she might be a little crazy.

"Mmmm. That feels good." Now she had her eyes closed.

He was rubbing her back. He was also thinking about where he
would sleep tonight. It would have to be the floor. The couch
was too narrow and his bed was out of the question. His bed? He
couldn't even call it a bed anymore. It was a mess of exposed

springs, torn fabric and cotton stuffing, but at least she hadn't gone after the pillows.

2 hours ago he had answered the door in a towel. She came in with a bottle of white wine and a black plastic bag. He had just gotten out of the shower, still wet, and Cassie's eyes were...well, her heart pumping, all that blood rushing, all those hormones being released, plus she had just finished her period.

"Hey honey."

She put down the wine, the plastic bag, made an attempt at her coat while he shut the door and couldn't do it (matter over mind), couldn't even say hello, she just grabbed him. They locked.

He managed her coat, her shirt. She whipped the towel off his waist and used both hands- all those hormones. They made it into the bedroom, Chicago naked, Cassie halfway there, fell onto the still undamaged mattress, and it was normal, good and healthy, the fireworks of foreplay exploding bright 4th of July...(I was at the job,

9:20 in the morning, watching this happen. And it's not like I was peeping or anything because Chicago always draws the shades, locks the doors, likes his security, and this was taking place in a small town on Long Island...I was in downtown Manhattan, miles, miles away...no matter, I still watched the whole thing and it was getting...)

"...so hot, Chicago, oh my god."

"Oh Cassie. You feel so..."

Naked now, displayed now and 2 hands per person not enough hands to cover all bases but somehow (inventive monkeys) humans get by. Some use feet, some use their vocal cords to stroke ears, some use hot breath to tingle necks, some use minds to create images and some use minds to think...

"Chicago?" now asking, not panting...minds to think.

"Yes?"

"Have you ever been with anybody on this bed?"

"What do you mean?"

She had never thought about it before. She'd slept in this bed, screwed in this bed, ate breakfast and masturbated in this bed while he was at work and never before did it…

"You know what I mean." pulling away, now eye to eye. "Have you ever fucked anybody in this bed? Besides me?"

"I don't know honey. Why does it matter?"

"Just answer me. Have you ever fucked anybody in this bed?"

"Well, yeah, I guess so."

She thought about it. Eye to eye. Cassie's got a good imagination and what she

imagines…

"You guess so? How many girls Chicago? Be honest."

"Two, maybe three girls, I really don't know honey."

"Don't know!"

She was out of bed, that good imagination firing and imagining two or three girls that he really doesn't know.

She was naked and jealous (right now Cassie's real jealous, the embodiment of,

the picture of, if you painted a picture-right now- of…her it would be just that one word scrawled across the canvas) and she was in the kitchen and Chicago got out of bed while she ran back into the room holding a knife.

↷ CHICAGO – PART 2

Cassie did a number on the bed. She stabbed at it, sliced horizontally, vertically, naked the whole time and Chicago didn't grab or try to stop her. He may have said something or muttered something, but mostly he looked at her ass. Also her thighs because they rippled with muscle and when she turned, the trimmed bush and pink nipples, just a man (matter over mind), a spring popped out from the mattress, nicked Cassie's thumb, the knife dropped, she yelped, a spot of blood and Chicago finally moved, went over to (scared of or for?) her.

"Cassie, honey, what're you doing?"

"How can you expect me to stay in that bed when you've had all those, all those…"

Tears and holding and questions. Soon the calm. It was the wine that helped. After a few glasses, Cassie explained while wiping at her nose.

"I just couldn't stand it. What if you thought about those girls when you were with me? Or maybe one night when I'm not around or something?"

And Chicago held her; kind of rocked her (baby Cassie), and she even called a phone number, spoke with a salesman, read the salesman the information off a credit card and was guaranteed that a new mattress would be delivered by tomorrow afternoon…(I also think that Cassie might be a little crazy, not a full-blown nutcase or anything, just a bit imbalanced. At my desk, in Manhattan, miles and miles away, the phone rings but I refuse to answer it. This is too entertaining. I could've stopped Cassie from destroying the mattress, but same as Chicago, just a man, got this appendage, Cassie's got a real good body on her and I wasn't about to miss out on…)

Chicago rubbing her back, they're not naked anymore, wearing t-shirts and sweatpants, the fire burning and Cassie's eyes closed…

"Mmmm. That feels good."

He pulled the t-shirt up around her ribs and rubbed her sides. Then he pulled the t-shirt up past her tits and rubbed her chest. Cassie moaned. Thrust out a little at the hips. The wine in the blood, the hormones in the body, on the couch she was squirming and the sweatpants had gone somewhere. No one really knows where they went- there one second, gone the next (I'm the dirty young man playing at god), and soon the two of them hotter than any log in any fire in any fireplace the world over…

"Oh Cassie."

Cassie, jealous as she was, imbalanced as she was, weak as she was, around Chicago, she was all woman and in bed she was all independent woman without a stitch of embarrassment, without a hint of inhibition, she actually spread her legs, grabbed Chicago's hand and sunk him to the third knuckle in more lava than wet flesh…

"Oh Chicago."

The fire burned, the flames high, (I can feel the heat from all the way over here, 11:30 in the morning, miles and miles…), sweating and the couch cushions itchy when you sweat and itchy when you're naked and sweating, also too much squirming around could mean rug burn on the ass, old couch, probably isn't all that clean, Cassie thinks, exactly how old is this couch? How long has Chicago had this thing for? Since college? Definitely. Maybe even before then and on the heels of that one thought, finger or fingers or no fingers whatsoever and third knuckle be damned…

"Chicago?"

"Yes honey?"

"Have you ever fooled around with anybody on this…"

Now they were on the floor. Chicago had spread out a sleeping bag in front of the fireplace and they lay side by side. In the fireplace was a couch cushion, the last of the 3 couch cushions, and it burned just as good, maybe even better (in Cassie's mind) than any old log would've burned. Except for the smell. A burning couch cushion just doesn't smell all that good but at least now they were warm again and close again and Chicago had never even had a girl touch his sleeping bag let alone gotten laid in the thing since it was used only for camping trips with his friends.

"I'm sorry I get so jealous Chicago. But it's just that I've grown to love you so much that..."

"Don't apologize honey, I know you love me. I love you too."

It's the truth. Chicago doesn't just love Cassie. He's in love with her, madly, has been since he first met her in high school over ten years ago. They had fooled around at 17, been together on and off throughout college and afterwards, but this was their first real go at a serious relationship.

"Just the thought of you with anyone else makes me crazy."

"Oh Cassie, don't worry about that, it's just you, always you, forever you hon…"

The smell had cleared out a little. (It was close to 1 o'clock in the afternoon and I had a meeting with one of my bosses. I wasn't sure what would happen while I was gone. I didn't want to miss a stroke, but I couldn't miss a paycheck…I had to let things happen on their own. I got up (away from my omnipresent point of view) from the desk in Manhattan…

…The meeting lasted over 2 hours. I checked back on the love scene and saw them smoking cigarettes in front of the fireplace. The couch cushion fire had died down, just scattered red embers and their faces content. Meanwhile I had a train to catch. The Blonde was picking me up at the station and I didn't want to keep her waiting.

I got there at 5:30- the station.

She had packed a bowl and we smoked on the ride home.

I was stoned, mind wandering, The Blonde was saying something but I wasn't in the car, at least not mentally, I was back with Chicago and Cassie. Now they were in the kitchen and Cassie was dressed, reaching into that black plastic bag she was holding when Chicago had first answered the door.)

"I wanted to give you something before I left. A present."

"Oh Cassie, you shouldn't have gotten me anything."

"Well, it's not just a gift for you, it's kind of something for me, too. To give me peace of mind."

"What do you mean?"

"Well, like this last week, when I had my period and all, I know you get horny and well, I just want you to be happy and not feel, you know, neglected or anything."

"Cassie, don't even think about that. I never feel..."

(The Blonde was saying something but I wasn't in the car. I was curious as all hell

and wanted to see what Cassie had in the bag.)

"Let me finish. So I went to a store today and bought something for you."

She pulls something out of the bag.

"What is it?" Chicago asked, even though he knew exactly what it was.

"What does it look like? It's a rubber mold of a woman's...you know."

"Yeah, I know, but why did you buy it?"

"That way when I have my period you can still..."

"But Cassie..."

"I even sprayed it with my perfume so that when you use it you'll..."

"I'm not going to..."

"But I want you to, I know how you get when I'm..."

(The Blonde was saying something but I wasn't listening, then she was yelling

something, I heard my name,

"John!"

"What!"

"I've been speaking to you for 5 minutes!"

"About what?"

"Damnit! Why don't you ever listen to me?"

"Why don't I ever listen to you? Damnit! Why haven't you ever bought me a rubber pussy?"

"A rubber what?"

"A rubber pussy with hairs and an asshole that I could..."

"John, what are you talking about? Why would you need a…"

"Forget it, forget it, I was thinking about something else."

And the car kept moving. The Blonde no longer talking. I thought about a rubber pussy while Cassie was walking out the door.) Chicago stood in the kitchen, working his finger in and out of one of the holes, then he brought the thing close to his nose and inhaled. It smelled just like her.

෬ CONFESSION

It helps to do this once every few months. Just sitting with a stranger; a person I've never met before, a person I hope to never meet again, and letting it all out. If I were religious, if I believed in something other than what I could touch or ingest via some orifice, then I'd probably be in a church. I'd be in that little booth throwing my guts at the face behind the partition. But god, the church, any church and any god just…Ah, I don't want to get into that right now. I don't want to get sidetracked.

"Mr. Duluth? Excuse me, Mr. Duluth?"

"Yup?"

"Doctor Bennet will see you now. Room number 12, right down the hall, it's the third door on your left."

I get up, find the room, get in and sit down. Number 12. Now I wait. I don't look around much because all these rooms look the same. Boxes of cotton swabs, gauze pads, tongue depressors, the rest, a long sheet of paper stretched across…I never get into those robes they give you. Those ridiculous things, open at the back…it's not the physical exposure that I'm after… About 10 minutes or so and I hear the doctor- G. Bennet MD., licensed by the great state of New York- outside the door.

He walks into the room holding a manila folder, a pen, wearing glasses, and reading over the forms I filled out in the waiting room, already making notes- all business. He sits down on the stool in the corner of the room, looks up at me and it's like the beginning of a boxing match, we're both in our respective corners, staring across the ring, a bell sounds...

"It says here that you're a smoker?"

"Ah, yeah. Smoker..."

"A man your age. You should really think about quitting Mr. Duluth."

"Smoker, drinker, drug addict. Ahhh, I never really thought much about quitting."

The doctor looks at me from across the examination room. Somewhat fazed by my opening flurry. His pen has stopped moving. It rests at the end of the last thing he's written, still pressed to the page, spreading ink like maybe he's imitating Rorschach.

"Criminal, cretin, lecher. Many labels have been affixed to my great I."

"Mr. Duluth?"

"I've been called a substandard citizen, a fence straddling idiot, and a full-fledged sex fiend all in one night."

"Mr. Duluth, surely this isn't..."

"I have outstanding warrants in three states. I've broken the hearts of good women and turned them sour as old milk. I've been calling in sick to work since the beginning of January and I'm waiting for the..."

"Please, Mr. Duluth, I don't need to hear all of this. You wrote here that you've been experiencing chest pains. Why don't we discuss that instead?"

That's his defense? The duck and move? Poor guy. A rabbit in a snare, a babe in the woods, easy pickings, a spectacled fish in a barrel and me with a BB gun…

"That's what I'm getting to Dr. Bennet. My chest pains."

I poke a finger into the layer of fat right above my heart.

"This is where I feel it the most. On the inside though. And mostly at night."

"At night?"

"Yeah, especially when I think about those two years where I thought I caught genital warts from that beautiful girl who wore a wig. Only I didn't know she wore a wig until the thing slipped off her semi-bald head and landed on my chest. Ha! Believe me, I was out of that bed and through the door the second I ca…"

"Warts?"

"Papules. They showed up three weeks after the wig hit my chest. I finally got the courage up to walk into that free clinic over in Hempstead and they checked me out. But for those two years, well…"

"Yes?"

"One night stands. At least twenty of them. Unprotected. Using names like Samuel Dalton, Crank Evans, Khaleeb Fahwazzy, thinking that if I infected enough people then maybe I could…"

"Could what?"

Hooked. A beautiful girl in a wig, genital warts and chest pains…this is what I came here for. Now Bennet wants to hear me out just as bad as I want to let it out, so I just look at him for a few more seconds without saying anything.

"Could what, Mr. Duluth?"

Hooked!

"So that I could wake up and walk around this place without feeling alone, like I wasn't the only one. It was like a connection or a bond, like finding someone that has the same birth date, name, tattoo as you do."

"I see."

"But then the tests came back negative and I was a free bird, absolved, and every now and then I would bump into a bouncing blonde, drunk brunette, fiery-crotched redhead from those two years and they would say, 'Hey Sammy-Crank-Khaleeb, how about a drink?', and I'd turn them down and walk away because I automatically thought they had warts."

"Ahhh, so the connection was a bad one even though you knew you hadn't infected them."

"Exactly!"

"And bumping into them forced you to think about what you were doing for those two years! When you thought that you really were infecting them!"

"Yes! That's it! Seeing them made me feel like a murderer."

"Even though all you did was sleep with them and move on?"

"It's the intention. The purpose behind my actions. Like I pointed a gun at them that I thought was loaded, pulled the trigger and walked away, left them for dead, you know? Only I found out later on that the bullets were really blanks."

"I see what you mean."

"Chest pains."

"Oh yes, your..."

Bennet snaps out of it, he looks back at the forms I filled out. I'm already standing up. I feel like I've lost weight, at least twenty pounds and I'm tempted to get on the scale in the corner of the examination room. I don't do it. Instead I begin walking out.

"Mr. Duluth?"

Down the hallway-

"Mr. Duluth?"

and through the waiting room-

"Mr. Duluth?"

then out the door, onto the street, I light a cigarette, inhale deep and exhale loudly, really savoring the taste of it. I roll them myself (Drum tobacco) and it's the difference between a good steak and a cheap burger. I look back over my shoulder, and see Bennet standing in the doorframe.

"Mr. Duluth?"

I nod at him.

"Chest pains?"

And I smile.

℘ I Wonder What She Called Me

I remembered thinking how it was like wrapping fruit trees so that they'd survive the winter,

which made me giggle

and she'd ask what was so funny while I hovered over her.

I threw myself at it like a task, like shoveling snow. I was laughing at a problem.

She did it too. It was all forced. And awkward.

And always the same. All the noises were artificial. She would do a great imitation

of a trout,

trapped on land and flopping, flopping, straining against the air.

A lot of the time it wouldn't come off.

For either of us.

We would wind up exhausted. Chafed. Out of breath and irritated

by the other's presence.

It ended

like these things usually end; badly, real sour,

but easy; not much yelling, just curses

and name calling, staring at each other, hating with more
emotion than we had ever found when undressed together.

In my head

I nicknamed her Cold Fish.

☙ HOT TUB THOUGHTS

little fat girls like my poetry

and broken housewives
with refillable prescriptions,

also fuckups
playing catch near cliff edges and

there's a couple
of drunks (in a fit of parentheses and those convulsive
morning
gut rot stomach cramps- kids raised by Buk,
that understand)…but to me…it's no dice, it's

old bread, it's holding your dick against the liquid
force of a whirlpool jet like

machine-made current's a
good girlfriend with all the right moves,
squinted eyes, I hear a voice,
'Some asshole's contaminated the damned Jacuzzi water!', while

I towel off,

dreaming
about the next line

෬ GOTTA GET OVER

This Dead kid (last night I saw

the deadest body

of all time no pulse, it was his eyes, no blood gushing main pump- heart

obviously

nothing left in the tank and no muscle moving

check pulse

same as gas gauge dead empty tank even it was in his eyes no fumes no good no sputter no jerk no good no nothing even

time of

involuntary

twitches gone past (did we get there late?) they were knocked out same as shoes

14 yr old

in socks, lying close to a tree like

he wanted it

picture perfect…its left me…(from a letter to Mike Green) unhinged…)

and so I pull a coke binge and see that the 900 dollar dog I opened the door for has gone AWOL and there's way

too much speed

to go to sleep

CR HE WOKE UP THINKING

Ah, good morning!

Hello, sweet daybreak!

Out of bed,

you slippery cunt,

to rinse your mouth

with warm vinegar.

CR THE REGULAR BAND

Friday night never happened due to black holes and
misfiring
synapses

but I begin to have second thoughts
when someone tells me

it really did happen

not only that

but
that it leaked into Saturday morning with
me
in the picture and I regained consciousness to find

myself

rubbing elbows with crack heads,
drunks, sluts and drug dealers, (((me!) the victim of) I had
snorted-drunk-smoked

enough

to intoxicate a schoolhouse of chubby children with high tolerances
and suicidal tendencies.) in a small bar

in a small town

while a band plays that same
old
song

℘ MAKING DEALS WITH...

I told him it was all flawed and
fucked up from the beginning. riddled with
inherent instabilities!
right from the design stage!
and he would smile,

once these wings are built I'll be able to...

but how can you call them wings?

like I was saying, once these wings are built I'll be able to fly most anywhere,

and away

from most anything that antagonizes, needles, anything trying to rape me on this round rotating...

but how can you call them wings?

you're pressing buttons, little keystrokes! and he'd smile like it was all teeth and stretched lip that made up his face, but each button pressed, little keystroke, is a flap of wing, one right and one left, equilibrium, a few more and...

I'm aloft...and then it would be my turn to smile, I'd make a noise that was half-snicker, half-contempt,

you seem almost crazy enough to make it work. okay,

you figure out how to get up there and I'll go with you, no questions asked, and

14 years later,

here I am,

little key strokes, and pressed buttons…aloft

CR MANHATTAN APPRECIATION

starving guitarists, bull-dikes, street vendors selling glass bowls, old t-shirts, used records and nose rings.

grayish reptile types with,

un-hinged jaws, with scales, rolling tongues, shedding layers of skin, smoking Newports.

all the subway stations, all the sewer tunnels.

all the airborne disease.

all the bloodied condoms in all the landfills of the world, all the teeth marks in rubber, all the saliva mixed with spermicide, all the…beauty that this city has to offer, all the…

children with runny eyes, noses, asses, chased by young lactating mothers stuffing napkins into their bras.

short skirts

floating

above fishnet stockings

with rips around the knee, with a sigh, with the creak of caked-on powder, with a history of bruised thighs, of alleyways, of strangers counting out bills on dumpsters and wooden pallets.

all the brown tap water, all the gurgling toilets.

all the bacteria on door knobs.

all the dreams of all the poets floating in all the cesspools of the world, all the words like old stool, all the bodily expulsions, all the…beauty that this city has to offer, all the…

confused tourists, checking maps, hailing cabs, asking directions in thick accents, using public restrooms and flying home with crabs.

stiff dicks

tucked

under straining belt buckles

with an awkward walk, with the real heavy breathing, a crowded elevator car where everyone gets jostled, bumped around, touched and felt up as they exit and enter.

all the clutter, all the madness.

all the spit on the sidewalk.

all the laughter of all the maniacs in all the psyche wards of the world, all the jokes like

stale bread, all that rotten taste in your mouth, ah, all the…beauty

that this city has to offer.

○R ON THE TRAIN RIDE HOME LAST NIGHT

Reading Plexus. Knocked off chapter 5 (hell of a thing) and had to sit back. Take it all in sort of speaking while looking out the window.

Then, staring at my reflection, I noticed my right eye looked pitch black in the LIRR plastic paned reflection and I started playing a game. Seeing how long I could focus on just my eye, just that right one.

I started with a 50 count, but couldn't get past 25. Second time around, I made it to 30. Fourth time 14, getting frustrated but curious at the same time I pushed on- 6, 7, 8 times and then finally, with magic number 9, I stumbled into an intense state of focus.

Not only could I concentrate on that dark as winter night with no street lamps on country back roads black eye, but without conscious effort, say, easy as Spanish maids parting curtains, I saw through all that black (and I've heard talk about things like 'the secret heart carried inside of each man', also 'the Third Eye that penetrates', but never before about the 'Secret Eyes', the ones concealed behind all that pupil and iris plus neural wiring business) and a mouth opened up in that Black Stone of the Kaaba, well cut onyx, mined obsidian orb of an eye and it told me,

'You're going to be famous.' It came with a twitch of an eyelid, a rise in heart rate, and I started sweating around the armpits…and then, from chest, left side (of course) an even louder voice, 'Get up! Run away! And, whatever you do, don't listen. Not yet.'

I jumped from the seat. I still had ten minutes before my stop but motion is motion, especially when dictated by furtive organs, things that develop inside of you without warning and speak up with Roman dictator-like authority…down the aisle, past old legs, shopping bags, briefcases, shoelaces, still far from my stop, all that interior chatter muted by the remote control of some Big Force, still shaken up, I stood by the exit doors, avoiding anything reflective.

CR POINTING FINGERS IN THE RIGHT DIRECTION

it's the weather that does it (discount everything else-
hookers and hotel rooms, nicotine
like oxygen,

enough beer to flood a small town- it's the weather)

it's the strong wind that forces you to shit blood, to puke
stomach acid, to pass out
in strange apartments

with a white ring
under your nose, and the rain, indecisive

December rain (liquid or solid) can't make up its mind,

and in the morning,

on the sidewalk, soaking wet,
with a pain in your stomach, you bet on a 3-dollar umbrella

from one of the Asian street vendors.

◯ LOOKING AROUND, QUESTIONING

where are all the pretty women

throwing flowers,
uncrossing legs,

where're all my friends,
my admirers,
my fans while I'm golden while glen danzig screams and I'm
full of light,
full of life,
full of special reserve 12 year old dewars,
full of smoke,
full of piss and vinegar and thunderbolts,
closer to thor than john,
closer to the clouds than the coffin, where the fuck

is everyone

at 1 o'clock, on a Friday

afternoon?

ॐ MY PRACTICAL FEET

moving through Penn Station rush hour

I'm playing in traffic

my sidewalk imagination

I'm being diagnosed

premeditated by who, on what level, (I'm thinking

it's somewhere

below

the everyday/run-of-the-mill/ho-hum type of subconscious that's riddling the brains of

all those

who've never dealt with

synthetic

shackle dream beds,

or lime green

explosive

acidic vomit

mornings…my body, your body, some body, the body a bag of

abnormal

activity, 'Scrape those flag waving bastards off the map! New state of action!

Police state of exposure! Place everything between slides,

toss them under a microscope, and bring in the Asians- Reverse

Engineering!

Figure out the weakest link in that old genetic chain! Then,

we'll apply the right kind of pressure

in all the right kind of places…') walking from Washington Square South

all the way down past Tribeca, past fashion, past cuisine, past manhole covers showing

broken

fingernails

(it's beginning to smell desperate) and red around the edges…kiddies, this city

was built

for a man of my nature

the right (synthetic shackle dream bed building and lime green explosive) kind of

guy doubling up on

vicodin and Milan Crème

brown hash at 7 am, and just yesterday

a tattooed man with stretched earlobes and a shaved head drops a hint, the location

of an old friend, 'I've been holding her in my apartment since 1995.' he tells me, then

making an offer, '15 dollars

for a quick peek

at your

warm

center.' but I (practical feet, lime green, bed shackles and all)

walked away…

Ꮽ MY WED MORNING RANT TO RIC
(MY HOTEL REVERIE)

a thousand lines of poetry
stands worthless in the face of
all this hotel room white
stucco ceiling tile- I've been here before

Peaks and Valleys

Downtime in the Dead City…(john says: hopefully things will
turn around- I've had tons of ideas, but not many lines, hundreds
of instances of teetering on the edge of all out laughter, but then
the situation diffuses in a snicker, orgasms turned into light
ejaculations, inevitably mad nights sputtering out in fits of
temporary insanity- there's a serious kink in the works, I'd say

Richard conrad says: wow

Richard conrad says: great piece

john says: yeah, and no solutions in sight, horizon grey with one
time champion flyers falling out of the sky like gnats that have
given up the ghost, the water too frothy and turbulent to provide
its womb like comfort,

john says: the city upstairs is in disarray, all my characters have
formed a mob and they're thinking mutiny, all my landscapes
smell like rubble, earthquakes through small towns, all

john says: the streets clogged with traffic, nothing but horns
honking and all the traffic lights busted out, everybody praying
for movement but not a one of them with the balls to stamp
down on the accelerator- downtime in the dead city, to say the
least

Richard conrad says: very nice…title?

john says: haha- my wed morning rant to ric

Richard conrad says: well, fuck! just like that? from the hip?

Richard conrad says: * clap clap clap clap *)…and then

Big Forces
bring down the curtains
and a cleaning lady
knocks at the door

◌⃝ Mamma-Mamma

give me pills that make me itch
that set me to nodding off during the day
only to leave me bouncing at night, pills that won't let me shit
for 5,
6,
7 days on end (bloated stomach, intestines
backed up with crap) and that let me get hard, but won't let me
come- oh,

Mamma-mamma make it so that I don't notice
traffic lights and round children
rolling like melons from school busses- swap
my brown eyes for black ones, glazed
and shot through with red- give my fingers
that shaking
jittery chemical clumsiness,

make it
so I can't handle a matchbook- oh
mamma give me ambition
playful
as unwanted kittens,
trapped
in a sack
at the bottom of a pond

CR THE ITALIAN'S GOT IT WRONG
(OR THIS EASY WEAKNESS)

through the stomach, my ass
it's through the balls
get a man
by the balls and the rest
is easy

CR POSTCARD FROM THE BAHAMAS

with The Blonde
throwing up
pesto noodles shivering, (while I type shit…)
with 3 bags of coke, a
bottle and a half of vodka on the beach on an alien continent
where (cab drivers are your best friends, your 'It snows in the
Bahamas' and I'm easy cornstalk in the right wind downfall)
with sun burnt skin in a rented hotel room with the nose on drip
with the brain flashing lightning 2000 thoughts an hour, how
else, could a john
of my caliber

relax

CR SEASONS GREETINGS

Sliding on ice white haired golden-oldies with bad hips

Chestnut children down the stairs crack open shells Tchaikovsky
melody

Drunk daddies swerving pine trees sliding off roof racks
swerving home

On the ladder with staple guns trip fall during decoration

Celebratory spirit captured at 50% off:

Red and green body paint

Snowflake pasties

Mrs. Cringle's little helper (stocky vibrator with elf's ears,

a single D battery- I'm thinking diamonds my ass!) paper cut's got gangrenous destiny

happy wrapped ending

tied bow tragedy warm under mistletoe a young man was grabbed

by a girl he'd never seen before (free clinic wish list!),

first outbreak a month later, redness around the lips,

widespread

old fruitcake induced indigestion, with the white snow

gone to dark grey, and a whole

new year

to screw up

ᠻᠣ SIMPLE SWAN DIVES FROM HIGH CLIFFS

sometimes it's so easy
you don't even try-

clumsy hands sweep a table,
knock over a bottle (and everything is reflex

everything is automated- is Domino Effect-
is wheels in motion- is Mouse Trap

by Milton Bradley

is the

inevitable pendulum...) and you scoop it up
before the foam
has a chance to rise- then real casual

you say something
outlandish
yet insightful that sets people to thinking, then smiling (and
there's laughter, more than what seems possible and it comes
from all around you) girls smile

as they walk by, touch you repeatedly when it isn't necessary
after striking up a conversation (kissed cheek hello- touched
hands, touched elbow, lower back, they bat eyes) those younger
than you,

or new in town, 'I heard you once drank the place out of whiskey
then beat hell out of 3 firemen.' and the regulars nod their heads,

give stamps of confirmation, jump into exaggerated memory, 'I
was there when it happened. He whooped their firemen asses
good. Tossed them right out that door over there and chased
them down the street. Took an hour to mop up the blood.'

but you never say a thing, just

(in that chemically detached
way of the 60's) smile

and climb a few feet higher

getting ready to jump.

ೞ PROBLEMS AND DREAMS

and dreaming of problems waking up to pillow cases packed
with coke to boots with thick hollowed soles packed with
vicodin, narcodan, oxycontin, a dream, waking up to faucets
dripping beer, scotch-whisky, absinthe, to backyards turned
poppy fields, turned pot fields, turned stretching desert vistas of
peyote cactus, a dream, waking up to all that hunger, all that
want, all that need, 6 am, wake up, empty two tall boys, a baby

suckling at some great alcoholic teat,
a john, a problem, I've got plenty,

I overdraw as much as the bank will let me and
go to work
on realizing my dreams

℞ SHADOWS COLLIDE (ACOUSTIC)

like something unheard of, never before imagined,
unclassifiable, or

maybe

like a golden, gleaming, shiny, damned futuristic age of music,
far advanced, sure,

I hear it,

feel something (like a kamikaze pilot coming in from over the
horizon (prepared

for the unknown!)) a shifting

inside

and upstairs, something calling me…it's the voice of the infinite,

it's destiny coming at me, it's a sound never meant
for mortal ears (yet I hear it,

and I'm afraid it'll blind me, turn me inside-out, shake the soul
from my body, leave me gasping

for…) this is what Big Forces would listen to,

this is something for the gods, only

1 question (while she yells,

'John, turn off that fucking racket!') why is it

(as I turn up the volume)

that I'm allowed to listen?

෨ THAT KID ON PULASKI

Yeah, I'm doing relatively well, as much as can be expected anyway. Coming home from a late night poker game, well out of my head, had just finished smoking and the normal beer intake, laughing, good music on the radio, and we (The Blonde, a friend, and myself) take a back road that's different from our normal route- what a move.

It was in conversation around the cards, one of the players says, "Take Pulaski down to RT25A. It's much faster and no cops."

and so of course...The Blonde behind the wheel while I play with the volume knob, the friend in the back (a well imbalanced brunette) is telling a story that I'm not listening to when The Blonde asks, "What's that?"

And I see, and laugh, saying, "It's just some chubby kid. But what the hell's he doing on the side of the road at 4 in the morning?"

The chubby kid; ha, I still call him the chubby kid and so do the rest of us that won the bad lotto that night.

We get closer and The Blonde's applying brakes, we finally see details, the chubby kid's face; (he's waving us down) white as milk, bone white, new baby teeth white but you could tell that it wasn't just his complexion. The Blonde drives by, more brake, open mouth, "We have to turn around. That kid needs help."

I second with a bad feeling rumbling around the gut area, the imbalanced brunette is "No, no, no, I don't think it's a good idea."

But by then we're U-turning across empty lanes (past 4 in the morning and not much traffic) and I'm out of the car much faster than I wish I was because chubby kid rolled-waddled-shuffled his meaty bulk over to me, "My friend's hurt. By the tree. Somebody hit him with…"

but I'm already (much faster than I wish I was) by the tree and looking; no shoes, clean socks, laid out, bad news, tan cargo pants worn down below the ass and a t-shirt un-tucked, arms at all the wrong angles, face, well, features, weren't a hundred percent because it was dark, also, real bloody…bad news.

I moved his arm, felt his chest, no luck, (and it wasn't just like he was sleeping- that's what I said to myself; it'll be just like feeling up some cute chick at a party that's passed out off Rufenol, Ketamine…the wrong idea.

It was rag doll dead weight that had no give and no spark, no tension, no nothing, no movement, nothing involuntary even) and then I put my ear to his chest, no luck, checked pulse at both wrists no luck, checked neck (that too, was at a shitty angle, all wrong from a skeletal standpoint) no luck, then shaking blonde next to me, shaking white chubby kid next to her, imbalanced brunette fidgeting in the dark, someone hands me a cell phone, "Just talk to them I can't do it."

EMT operator asks "Is there a pulse?"

"None, I checked everywhere, I don't think there's any…" (I'm almost hysterical)

"Just calm down Sir. Do you know CPR?"

"Yes."

Looking down though, when she asked me that, I caught eyes for the first time and understood it was green pastures, clouds, harps maybe, who knows, it was something out of reach-

"Do you want to try giving the boy CPR?"

And I looked, wiped blood off the kid's mouth, that shitty angle of neck- "No. I don't think he needs that."

"Are you sure Sir?"

"Yes, he doesn't need that, call this kid's family, get professionals out here…"

Eventually the police, the ambulance, notepads and questioning the chubby kid, The Blonde taking names (a cop trick to calm nerves when they pulled up and saw us, all of us white and all of us shaking, stupid lost lambs) and I walked away, back to the car, to wait it out.

I stood pissing by the front left tire, but got most of it on my pants. Smoked cigarettes that bounced like a laser light show-burning cherry in the dark, bad hands, bit of a mess) and then somehow we were home.

Pacing around the kitchen drinking beer and stirring a pot of Manhattan clam chowder. It was a hell of a big pot too. I used 2 cans of that condensed shit on sale last week at the Stop and Shop. Also a large can of 'Pre-Shucked and Diced Clams' that had a thick layer of dust around the lid.

I made enough to feed a large family. Added spices; paprika, black pepper, a little oregano, tasted it, a little salt, it was good, resourceful chef and all that I am- but The Blonde wants nothing to do with clam chowder and neither do dead kids nor their chubby friends. I ate two bowls of it and then tossed the rest into the trash. That was it. I really didn't see any reason to put it in the fridge.

☞ TRUMPET SOLO FOR THE BLUES

young girls wearing blue dresses

young girls in the park

young girls scribbling disjointed
lines in spiral ringed notebooks,

on a Westbound train, there's a soft voice 'Tickets. All tickets please.'

young girls (almost singing, 'Tickets. All tickets please.
Excuse me sir,') saving paychecks and living in small
one room
apartments ('ticket please.'

'Oh,

sorry. Just a minute.' ((shaken out of my
Westbound

trance) fumbling for the ticket, finding it, looking up, into the
face of

yet another
young girl) 'Thank you sir. Tickets. All tickets please.' as she
moves
to the next car.) and of course

all these
young girls
have been raped
abused
burned by something that stays
fresh in their memory

far beyond
the actual

incident…all these young girls

on lonely Thursday night- Macaroni and Cheese is just fine

when Mr. Right
is never there

settling down on the couch

to stroke at a fat tabby

ⳏ I Could've Been

an avant-garde architect, trapping the

nightmares of the future

in arches, columns, I'd ride a donkey at a young age, kind of

like Gaudi

❦ THE OLD ASIANS CLAP

talking shop, primarily, musty old pile fit for a sow

so much rotten sausage, apple core, milk in the sun, green egg, melon rind

long time sleepers (dreamless, of course) reanimated, forced back into the dance hall

also used condom, found during spring clean-up

summit of stomach fluid yellow mountain, green bird tight-wire act

(big forces don't smile down on the headfirst reckless bit, they're Japanese patient, 'Little bird, if you do not sing, I will wait for you to sing…') green bird composer, perched

on cherry freckled flag post

above cherry freckled flag (hangs limp, even in the strongest of wind)

lets out
three
clever notes,

then flies

❦ THE WORST IS

the worst is

11 o'clock or so

on a Monday

night, alone

in bed, empties lining the headboard,

displayed on bookshelves like trophies;

bowling

baseball

hockey

trophies, the mattress; stains, ashes and

cigarette burns, the air smoky, a television sits

in the background, and in your head

you try to think of your accomplishments,

any accomplishments, anything at all,

but instead you come up with debts;

social

emotional

financial

debts and you notice that you're laughing, it's

the laugh of the hopeless, while

wondering

how the hell

you'll ever make it.

◲ THE IQ TEST – PRETENSION, ANALYSIS, A NICE LITTLE STORY...

I get the email telling me that I'm a Creative Theorist. It says, 'Creative Theorists are highly imaginative and excel at being innovative and conjuring up notions of what could be.' The email asks, 'Want to learn more about the way you think?' 'Want to find out how you can boost your brainpower?'

I'm not quite sure that I do- heavy-set, walking across thin ice, I can almost hear rushing water underneath me... The pitch: email lets me know, special, limited time only, discount offer, $9.95

and I get my very own, personalized, tailor cut and fit, custom designed Super IQ Report that'll teach me more about my thinking style, help me to discover the logic behind my subconscious reasoning, find the career path that's right for me, reveal the sources of stimuli for my unconscious mind, increase my penis size by 2-5 inches, expose the weaknesses in my personality and instruct me on exercises that will strengthen everything from short-term memory to my rectal fortitude. And all for $9.95. But I don't go for it.

I had answered the 58 questions some time last week. My sister told me about it. She took the test and scored pretty well, 137. Only 1 person out of every 100 scores a 137. I pulled 126, I'm 1 out of 19, I'm in the top 5.2 percent and that's fine by me, hell, Lincoln was just above 150, Einstein 160, and past that, well, past that we're talking Shakespeare, Goethe, Newton...only 1 in a 1,000,000...not a John in the crowd. 9.95? Not out of my pocket.

Hell, I'm a college educated Creative Theorist with pharmaceutical inclinations, social anxiety disorders and an outstanding bar tab... qualifications! I should be able to figure it out on my own.

Plus, I'm more than content with my penis; it's proportionate to the rest of my body, has a fine looking face with an admirably placed eye, a well outlined urethra, can spit over 4 feet when manipulated correctly, solves Samsonian-like riddles of the vagina with ease, is capable of computing the toughest of pubic algorithms in a matter of a few, toe curling, pre-ejaculate seconds, can detect a teenager in heat across a distance of 4 city blocks...a veritable divining rod of a cod if there ever was one... 9.95? Good luck WebIq!

So now I consider myself to be a Creative Theorist! Sure. 126. Fine! It means that I'm smart enough to know that there's something seriously wrong with the big picture. That there's something out of whack, a chink in the chain, a gear with chipped teeth, a frayed belt, a loose roller, a distinguished monkey conductor, asleep in the orchestra pit, dreaming of bananas while the crowd masturbates in the theater, 'We brought our tickets! We expect our entertainment!' The cock-struck young usher shuffling between rows, carrying a flashlight, hand lotion and a hidden camera taped to the inside of his coat sleeve… A Creative Theorist knows.

A Creative Theorist can foretell the potential outcome of small ripples making their way across the face of a lake. He can pinpoint boulders along the shoreline that will eventually be eroded by those small ripples. A Creative Theorist looks at those boulders and can't help but see their skipping stone eventuality…damned Creative Theorist, poor, confounded, spider web bound Creative Theorist…guy will always see the skipping stone, but never a way to rescue the boulder, never a final solution.

For a Creative Theorist, there's only the temporary fix…cheaply patched tires, cracked chair legs bound in duct tape, bubble gum used to plug a small leak in the wall of a great dam…aaaghhh, guy will try to mend a broken arm with aspirin and an ACE bandage- fantastic!

A Creative Theorist falls into the Catch-22 category of mental classifications. With all that insight and imagination, with all that intellectual disposition, a Creative Theorist can surely discern what the problem is, but is limited- restricted, held back, kept under cerebral wraps, is logically fucked over- by the confines of his acumen. The Creative Theorist's brain never allows him to reach a final solution; it only grants him enough vision to see the problem…upstairs, like a snake gnawing at its tail.

The Creative Theorist, after enough time and consideration, reaches this conclusion, yells, "I'm screwed! That's it! Perpetually! Undoubtedly! Irreversibly fucking…" guy sighs, thinks for a moment and asks, "Okay, so what's left? (He's run out of footholds while climbing a mountain, hanging by a pinky, he looks down) Any chance of salvation?" guy gets upset, becomes lyrical when faced with life's death- sentence…remembers forgotten physical dreams, "Does the island in the distance with the dancing girls in grass skirts and coconut cups that continually slide off of their tits really exist?

Will there ever be ripe coconuts falling at my feet from trees that stretch towards the sun? Will there be fresh lobster, large and kicking, Caribbean yellow claws, caught daily and served up next to molded balls of rice in the style of the native Indians that inhabit the island Kuanidup?"

I doubt it.

What's left is a pile of unanswerable questions, a never-ending list of unresolved issues, some huge and cosmic bucket of stripped screws, rusty cogs, bent cotter-pins and not a tap and die set, let alone a working set of pliers or a can of WD-40 in sight. Salvation? For a Creative Theorist? Escape? Anything short of the crematorium, a yawning burial site, the frenzied beeping of hospital monitoring equipment, a good length of rope and a sturdy roof beam, or a ten point swan dive off the tallest building in Manhattan won't cut it.

As for the island in the distance, well, I've been to Kuanidup. I ate the fresh lobster and the molded rice balls. I drank white Secco rum from a gallon jug with the Indians. Felt up my girlfriend for an hour before falling asleep in a thatched hut alongside translucent ghost crabs and fleet-footed green geckos.

I even woke up at 5 in the morning, hung over and retching onto the immaculate white sand, to watch the sun rise. I saw flocks of pelicans, 7-foot wingspan tearing hell out of the morning sky, settle onto the turquoise water, fill their beaks with small squid, fish and shrimp, then return to perch atop those stretching trees that I only dreamed would exist somewhere...out in the...out past all...beyond the skyscraper studded skyline, billboards, old factories with endlessly smoking chimneys (what the hell are they always burning in there?)...

And for a tiny, baby minute, surrounded by all that water, white sand, proud standing trees and prettily perching animals, just for a minute, blink of an eye type minute, I thought that I had beaten the system, Creative Theorist that I am, Mr. 126, Mr. 1 out of 19, Mr. look at my Rubix Cubic; it's got all the colors lined up...!

Amazing. I actually believed that somehow, in some roundabout and back assed way, that I had stumbled onto the final solution.

Maybe during one of my blackout sessions? And then one of the Indians, he was called Bee-Bee and I had played lots of beach volleyball with him, wearing a sun faded t-shirt that showed the smiling face of Winnie the Pooh, started loading the dugout canoe that would take all us tourists, weekenders, get-awayers, Creative Theorists, quick-fix artists, sure, back to the mainland that afternoon.

✿ UNDERBELLY OF THE MELTING POT

old and dusty,

old-time tunes on sun burnt records, love songs with strong hands

wound round their necks, choked out

on Manhattan

subway cars,

also

religion (Buddha and the good book) from all corners and the caffeinated

eyes

on the newspaper people, loud gin rummy guys yelling cunt over bad cards, guys plagued with bleeding, sleepy wives and too much

imagination

staring at the young girls dressed for a big day in the city, black women

in heavy

bright neon space-aged green

felt hats, and advertisements for Godiva chocolates showing semi-

nude heroin chicks with rape on the back-brain and no littering,
no smoking, no radio playing,

and you aren't supposed to lean on,

or hold the doors,

even if it's some grandmother

hauling ass

in varicose veins lugging ripped shopping bags with coat hanger
handles sporting

a goat's beard and a white film

over

her once bright

blue right goat's eye, rats when you step off

remind you to watch the gap, and you head towards the daylight

wondering what it's like

above ground

○ WHAT HAPPENS IS

you find yourself crumpled up, paralyzed, the wind knocked out
of you while

laying
at the bottom of the stairs and then it hits you

that you may have
just

fallen

CR WORSE THAN POISON IVY

undeniable itch when
far reaching forearm- bottom of the barrel itch when
drugstore
cowboy- end of the line-
fantasy
when
pleading phone calls IOU's when
-lion trainer looks scared, trusty whip snapped in two
-old man pulls on a rope, empty bucket out of a well
-bank machine giggles, Insufficient Funds
-running on fumes, jerk-shudder-tremble, car comes to a halt,
'No fuel
this side of legal
will ever get that engine
turned over'

CR UNTITLED

with my hand down the back of her…

like being at the beach
like jumping from a plane
like laying in the bathtub

drinking tall
bud cans

while unfastening hooks…

I sifted sand through my fingers
fell to the earth at a hundred
twenty something miles an hour

submerged my head and blew bubbles
pretending to be a seahorse

then my mouth was around…
cracked grey shells, seaweed, tasted salt and
ran out of air

moved lower towards…

big sun, mowed grass, feet along the rocky bottom

then kicked off towards the blue
-suntan lotion, an emergency chute, water wings, even a snorkel
-skin cancer, a bad fall, 'I think I see something down near the
bottom. Was he wearing blue trunks?' (lots to cry over)

"Are you ready?"

"Yeah. Are you?"

"Just start it, then I'll roll it the rest of the way down."

"Ok, do you want the top?"

"It doesn't matter. Whichever way is fine."

now fire, always the sun, always the grass, but only now fire, the
rocky bottom
not as far down as it looks

small pebbles
caught between toes

pieces of flecks of spots of green glued to fingers

moles misbehave, act up during examinations, are called
abnormal and sent to detention centers, lifeguards

climb down from high posts, lawn boys
pack up landscaping trucks, the bathtub drained, swirling
empties, Coriolis clockwise current, a match flares, wink one

then wink the other, the easy exhale, the spermicidal detachment,
I just now

noticed television, channel 5,
also that your knee

is blocking the screen

❧ I Could've Been

a Nobel winning scientist

the guy who came up with a pill that

put women in heat and

even made them

agreeable

❧ We Were Lying On The Beach

We were lying on the beach. It was August. The 22nd.

Under the last hour or so of sun that was left in the Bahamian day we read and mixed vodka with juice because all the beer was imported and cost over 40 dollars a case. Vodka always ripped my stomach apart, but it cost only 7 dollars for a big bottle and the juice was 2.

Every few minutes one of us would dip our heads into the open book bag that sat between us, turn up our noses with a curse of speed, and ask the other, 'Am I all right?'

The Blonde was absorbed in a magazine. *People*, *Stars*, who knows, some rag filled with airbrushed photos and celebrity gossip.

I was playing the literary snob, halfway through *In Dubious Battle*, and with all that white in my brains…I emptied the plastic cup and grimaced at the acid that I could feel building up in my guts.

"Do you want another one?"

"No, I just had one. It's pretty strong."

"I meant another drink."

"Oh."

"Well?"

"Sure, but not so heavy on the vodka this time. I think it's starting to get to me."

"It's this sun."

The ice bucket from the hotel room was down to cold water and a few stray cubes. I fished out the cubes, measured out 3 shots of liquor per cup, and mixed in some juice. I handed The Blonde her drink.

"Look at my towel."

There was a cartoon sun on the towel. I had bought it at the gift shop in the lobby of the hotel. Beneath the sun was some junk dreamed up by some tourism bureau. It proclaimed the beaches in the Bahamas to be blanketed by the finest sand, and warmed by the strongest sun, to be found the world over. The Blonde nodded her head in agreement.

"It sure is strong."

"Yeah. This sun is serious business. At first I thought the towel was lying, but I guess not."

"I meant the coke. My whole face is numb, but I am sweating pretty bad."

"Oh. Me too."

"Should we go in the pool?"

We stood up with an energy that was more chemical than natural, and made our way over to the pool. Hotel management had placed buckets of water around the pool. You were supposed to dip your feet into the buckets to get the sand off.

We took turns helping each other balance on one leg, and then made a run for the pool. The Blonde sat on the ledge before slipping into the blue. I made an attempt at a jackknife and hit chest first. I came up blowing bubbles.

"Did you see that dive?"

"No, I was underwater, but I heard it."

"I think it might've been a triple lindy."

"A what?"

I inhaled and submerged myself again. Then I swam over to the shallow end where I saw The Blonde's legs.

"Ow! You bastard! You just bit me!"

"Sharky's Revenge!"

She was rubbing at the back of her thigh.

"That really hurt."

"I'm sorry honey. C'mon, let's get out and smoke a butt."

We walked back to the beach. I dried my hands and lit 2 cigarettes. I looked over and saw The Blonde's head, wrapped turban style in a towel, disappearing into the book bag. She came up with a curse.

"Ho-Shit! Who would think we'd be able to get coke this good here."

It was the cab driver. On the way to the hotel from the airport he had turned to us with a smile when we told him we were from New York.

"The Big Apple mon! You like to party? Everybody in New York likes to party! You want some smoke? Maybe go skiing?"

His black face exploded with laughter as he turned back to the road.

"Anything you want. You just let Sammy know. Ha-Ha! It snows here in the Bahamas! Snows!"

We exchanged looks in the back of the cab. The Blonde shook her head and mouthed the word 'Cop', but I didn't think so. You deal with enough of these guys and you eventually get a feel for it. Or at least you told yourself that you got a feel for it until you were arrested.

The Blonde sipped at her drink.

"I'm surprised we didn't get ripped off."

"Nah, that guy was okay. I could tell."

"Did you think about what you want to do for your birthday yet?"

In 2 days I would turn 28. I didn't like it, but I couldn't do anything about it. Anything rational anyway. I picked up my drink.

"I don't know. We could swim with dolphins. Take the booze cruise. Anything."

"Well think about it and let me know. Whatever you want to do is fine with me."

She picked up her magazine and I jumped back into *Battle*. I read a few paragraphs. Then I knocked off my drink and thought for a while.

I watched the sun submit to its orbit and the waves give in to the pull of the moon.

I felt myself (so small and inconsiderable in the celestial scheme of things) accepting the whims of ego.

"You know, I think I'd give my left leg if I could write only half as well as Steinbeck."

"What are you talking about?"

"Read this sentence. Here. The one about the dogs."

"Shit."

"Yeah. It's serious business. More serious than the sun even. I don't think I'll ever be able write a sentence like that."

Then I sunk my head into the book bag. I came up and tilted my head so The Blonde could see up my nostrils.

"Am I all right?"

"Yeah. I don't think I'd like it if you wrote like Steinbeck."

"Me neither, but he sure knew what he was doing."

"So do you."

"Nah, I only think I know what I'm doing. Most of the time it's guess-work."

"Well I like the way you write. Fuck Steinbeck!"

"What?"

"I said 'Fuck! Steinbeck!"

"What about 'Pastures of Heaven'?"

"Never read it."

"Then how can you…"

The last few days in the sun had left our skin brown and appealing in a way that New York just didn't know how to do. She turned on her side and looked at me. I caught a glimpse of white skin when the top of her bathing suit shifted with the motion.

"Stop measuring yourself up to these guys. It's always Fitzgerald, or Faulkner, or Dusty whatever the fuck his name is-I don't like it. You've gotta stop doing it."

I reached out with my index finger and touched the strip of white on her chest. Then I put the finger in my mouth. I closed my eyes, savoring the taste of salt, chlorine, suntan lotion and skin.

"See that, I don't think Steinbeck would've done something like that."

"I bet we'd glow if we were naked and the lights were off."

"I'm serious John."

"So am I."

"Okay, let's make a deal."

She smiled and a sleepy, sensual look took over her face.

"We can go see if we glow on one condition."

My tongue rolled over in the taste. I noticed that my finger was slowly inching back towards that strip of white skin. She grabbed my hand.

"On one condition."

"What's that?"

"I don't want to hear anymore about those guys. No more Dos Pasos, no more Huxley, or Kosinski, none of them."

"How about Miller?"

She moved with a feline quickness, her hand going to the bulge in my bathing suit, gripping me in an only somewhat playful manner. Her eyes flashed and changed.

"If you even mention Miller, just once, I'll squeeze your…"

We packed up the towels and the book bag and the ice bucket. There was a narrow path leading from the beach back to the hotel and I let her walk in front while I watched the roll of her thighs and ass beneath the multicolored bathing suit bottom.

◌℞ THE EEL IN A HAMMOCK

while the wretched, the dreamless, the responsible, shit-for-
brains, key punchers

wrestle
with keyboards, serving trays, hem-lines, account ledgers I'm

suspended, smoking joints in
a purple hammock, while

there's bustle and strain and overtime being clocked I
drink beer by the 6, by the 12 pack, by the case, by the river,
suspended

in a purple hammock, while my bosses leave voice mail, send e-
mails, circulate memos, organize search parties, rig traps in
the tall sea grass I'm

suspended, hanging, 5 feet above ground, The Eel;
the delinquent, the deserter, the no-show, the walk-out, the waif,
fugitive

of a hundred
institutional

sea-
scapes,

I'm that slippery

and managerial search parties, traps
in tall grass be damned, it's
awful hard

to catch an eel

○ऽ WE WERE IN A CAR

(We were in a car. The Blonde was driving. I was staring at the
dashboard.)

"What are you thinking about?"

"Nothing"

An 85-year-old woman (the smile of senility, in a white dress)
standing over an imagined subway grate with the air blowing
up…

"It doesn't look like you're thinking about nothing."

"I am."

Peaceful, like bridges with no cars, sure looks nice without
having to see all that shit being shuttled back and…

"You know, sometimes I look at you…"

"And?"

The blonde stubble on her knee caught at the hair on my throat
as I was using little kisses to bring her…

"It's like you're somewhere else, like you're not even sitting
here."

"Where else would I be?"

Fingering the jukebox, it was an act of pure seduction, the buttons lit up, it was one of her favorite songs, that melody sounds so…

"I don't know where you are. You tell me."

"I'm right here kitten, in the passenger seat, rolling a cigarette."

"That's just where your body is, but your head, your head is somewhere else."

"All right, my head is in a nursing home. I'm watching an old woman pretending to be Marilyn Monroe."

"Okay."

"My head is 50 feet above the Whitestone Bridge that time it was closed for repairs."

"Whatever."

"My head is also in that hotel, The Hunter Arms, you remember it? When you forgot to shave that patch of hair off your knee."

"You're crazy."

"No I'm not, I just work differently from you. And my head is in the bar from last week, when you were playing with the jukebox."

"What about it?"

"You had your finger in your mouth, maybe you were biting your nails, and then you pressed the buttons real slow, and then the buttons were all shiny like there was saliva on them."

"I didn't do that."

"Yeah you did. You fingered the jukebox. I was watching you."

"Whatever."

"You seduced it. And then it played Wild Child for you because it was satisfied."

"I think I liked it better when said you were thinking about nothing."

"Sleeping dogs honey."

"Yeah. I should know by now."

(She was wearing a brown skirt. I looked at it. I started jumping forward, 3, 4, hours from now. I would be lying on my back. She would be standing over me.)

Playing at Fall, I reached up, pulled a string and down came all the dead leaves of the year, I saw two pale branches

and where they met...

Ꮧ ENTREPRENEURS

I looked around the van. There were six of us, sitting on two benches, three to a bench, facing each other, in the back of the van. Everyone's face nondescript, but young, I could say that. We all wore yellow rain jackets and hardhats that had been spray-painted red. A bottle of alcohol was being passed around. It came to me and I took a long swallow. Then I took a second one.

From the front of the van I could hear static and jabbered fragments of words coming from a police band scanner. I passed the bottle to my left, looked around, took inventory; there were garden hoses coiled up in a corner, shovels hung from hooks, I counted; four buckets filled with sand, two pickaxes, one guy lifted his leg, let out a sound- high pitched sputtering of released gas through a somewhat constricted orifice- and the gang all laughed.

"Alright boys, we got one!"

It came from the passenger seat; another guy in a yellow rain jacket and spray-painted hardhat, he rummaged around the floor, came up with a red pulsing strobe light that he placed on the dashboard, and the van picked up speed.

We pulled up in front of a small house in a small neighborhood and jumped out through the back doors of the van. The house was on fire. Not bad, it wasn't blazing just yet, but it was getting there. Immediately two of the guys had uncoiled two garden hoses and were stumbling around on lawns, stomping through flowerbeds, tangling legs in hoses, falling down, rolling onto their stomachs, yelling 'Emergency!' and popping up with hats cocked to the side, giggling, looking for faucets to connect the hoses to.

Two other guys grabbed shovels and buckets of sand, they ran towards the burning house, off balance with the weight of the buckets they collided into one another and fell about twenty feet from the front door. They threw rocks through the windows, shoveled the sand off the lawn, ran and pitched it in through the busted panes of glass. The guy that was in the passenger seat hopped out and started walking in circles around the burning house with a hand cupped to his ear; he listened for the mewling of kittens, the yelping of pups, the gurgles and cries of babes forgotten in the flames.

The driver moved slowly, he was a big guy, round and pudgy, well overweight, a donut's distance away from obese, his rain jacket couldn't be buttoned, his body heaved, surged, spilled out of the van and he just stood there holding a baseball bat, brushing at crumbs, digging at his ass and smelling his fingers before biting at the nail…in black magic marker the word Chief was written on his hardhat. Mixed with all this was a gaggle of neighbors with craned necks, flapping wings, neighbors with questions on their faces, milling around, looking anxious, confused, and beaks full of questions like:

"Who the hell are you people?"

"What are you doing?"

"Why is that man trampling through my rose beds, my azaleas, my peonies, irises and big-faced sunflowers?"

"Should we call the police?"

I reached for a pickaxe just as the hoses were connected, the water turned on, and turning away from the van I saw a string of flashing lights, heard tires screeching, a siren wailing, braying, screaming loud and bright both at the same time and moving fast, turning the corner, pulling up right alongside the van.

Real firemen jumped down from atop the truck and through the doors real organized and outfitted with real uniforms, looking pissed off, they split up in groups, one group moving towards the guys with hoses, another group moving towards the guys shoveling sand, one group after the Chief, one group following in circles the guy walking in circles with his hand cupped to his ear, and one group came after me and my pickaxe just as I was punching a hole through the front door.

It was one hell of a scene. The Chief, as big and round as he was, as packed to the brim with pizzas and chicken pot pies as anyone could be, filled with buttered rolls, banana breads, crab cakes, no longer digging, sniffing, or biting at his nails, but swinging the baseball bat with precision, connecting with heads, midsections, knocking out front teeth, cracking ribs, laughing the whole time, cursing the city, the state, the governor and mayor, while yelling instructions and precautions to the rest of us, 'Watch out on your left Sammy! Duck!' 'They're coming up behind you Mikey! Use your shovel!' 'Move out of that doorframe John! They're trying to box you in!' That's why he's the Chief.

Sammy ducked just in time and then came up with the hose spraying the firemen in the face. Mikey turned around fast, using momentum to power his swing, and knocked a few of the firemen aside with the steel end of the shovel. I jumped out of the doorframe just as an axe head landed. It bit into the wood where I was standing less than a second ago. I jabbed the flat head of the pickaxe into a stomach, heard a snap and kept moving.

The house was in a full blaze. The area around it was getting noticeably hotter. Firemen and vigilantes, a few of the neighbors, as well as the house owners; bleeding, hurt, laying in piles, trying to defend themselves, some screaming, others crawling off the battlefield/front lawn, trying to get back into their vehicles or onto their properties.

By the time I made it back to the van and dropped onto one of the benches the house was gone, consumed, burned down to the foundation. The Chief was in the driver's seat with blood running from a cut somewhere under his hardhat. One by one the rest of the guys showed up, cradling arms, favoring legs, limping, groaning, some no longer wearing their hardhats, some with ripped rain jackets.

In the Emergency Room the Chief, slurring and with gauze wrapped around his head, gave a speech.

"You did a damned fine job tonight boys. You kept your heads on, and you worked hard. I'm proud of you. Real proud. And I don't want you guys getting discouraged. We gave it our best shot tonight, but we can't expect to win every time."

The Chief paused. He looked lost, a little drunk, maybe dizzy from the blow he had taken. I came to his rescue.

"It wasn't a fair fight boss. Tonight it seemed like they had an army of guys on that truck, plus all those neighbors. One woman was hiding in the bushes, when I ran by the crazy broad jumped out and bit the back of my neck."

"I saw that Johnny, she was a rabid bitch alright. Old too. From now on you know to look out for those biddies; blue hair is the giveaway. But what I want to say to you guys is that you shouldn't be upset over what happened tonight. You have to understand that what we're doing takes time. It takes patience, blood, grit. You have to understand that the world has been closing in on itself for a long, long time now, that there's barely any room left for entrepreneurs like us."

The Chief paused again; he looked down at his shoes, like he was either finished speaking or trying to collect his thoughts. After a span of some uncomfortable time the Chief swept over the group with his eyes.

"This isn't the first time we've had our asses licked like this. And we can expect to get licked again, but remember, brave Daedalus never once thought of an airplane before taking to the skies, and AIDS was just the dream of a virus before man conquered the shark. Remember that boys. I'll see you all tomorrow."

✿ Redecoration, Confusion, The Great Pharaoh Dempsey On His Throne!

Woke up Sunday morning (the usual shell of a husk of a kid more prescription pill bottle than actual, more alcohol receptacle (like maybe I'm a skin and bone tumbler, pitcher, pint glass) than actual, more zombie in need of a shave than an actual kid), and it's the year 2007 and even zombies get email:

Congratulations- You are the winning bidder of item #5385806097 Egyptian Throne / Chair of Sitamun…wait, you know how jumpy I am (When you type or as you breathe? Huh Johnny? Both!), and I started somewhere in the middle of this thing and that's not really the right way to do it and…

so…

This place I'm renting with The Giant. He's got a fixation; pictures, paintings, posters, a decorative kid and all and there's nothing wrong with that, it's fine, pictures, paintings, and posters…but they're all of horses; oils on canvas of the Kentucky Derby in motion, a black and white of some- at one time family owned- runner named 'Journalist', a 4 foot long banner yelling "Preakness '94!" above a doorway, a poster stolen from the race track announcing the 'Belmont Spring Fantasy Challenge' and signed by people I've never heard of, and at first, looking around, I thought:

Alright, I've known this kid for a while, his family used to have money, a stable, he told me that when he was 7 or so his father used to make him shovel all the shit out of the stables and how this one time he spooked one of the horses and the thing kicked him square in the chest.

Says he wound up on his back. Sinking into a pile of shit, hitching for breath, crying, he pissed himself, scared that the horse was gonna trample him…says it took two years before he could look at a horse, even from a distance, without shaking... Seems he got over it.

So all these pictures, paintings, posters of horses, of horse races and horse related events and I'm looking around…all of a sudden, late Friday night, it hits me: I'm living in a temple dedicated to equine worship! Veneration! Adulation to such a point it reminds me how in Jersey there's no law against bestiality but 'Love Thy Neigh!' be damned, this is New York…I stumbled into my bedroom.

In the bedroom I got down to boxer shorts (Why all those horses?), and laying down, fiddling with the head of my dick, I tried thinking about The Blonde; in 3 different positions (trot, cantor, gallop) while playing tug of war with my abdomen, (hooves, teeth and tail) imagining myself cheek deep in pale mountains (colts, fillies and foals), pretending to disturb a small man in a canoe with my tongue (saddles, spurs and a bit)…I was about to spit into my palm (corrals, paddocks, stalls- I was trapped!), but was smart enough to realize it wouldn't work (my pubes would've been a mess of saliva and there wouldn't be an inch of responsive…) I just couldn't stop picturing horses…

So in comes Saturday. I had spent most of my day snorting Narcodan and nodding off in my hammock. I had also drawn spider webs on both elbows, colored my right pinky nail with black magic marker, tried to type a poem but wound up sipping straight Dewar's out of a tall glass like a real refined gentleman (John, the polished and cultured kid, standing at the helm of a sailboat, white sailor's cap on my head at a slight angle)…but, in my defense, I had run out of soda the night before.

By 7 pm I was ready to tackle whatever the night would bring. First it brought The Blonde, and she thought I was in fine form. I knew this because she took out her cell phone and switched it to picture mode as I rolled out of the hammock and landed on my back. (Sometimes I think she's putting together a documentary. (Something unseen asks, 'Ego?')) And The Giant says,

"He's been at it all day."

"I can tell."

But I bull-rush her. Kiss her about fifteen times on the neck, forehead, and chin, make her giggle and squirm away. As she heads towards the fridge for wine I light a butt and sit on the couch. I look around the place, wondering why I haven't left my room all day, and then remember: the horses. All those damned horses, and I don't know how, but they seemed to have multiplied at some point when I wasn't paying attention.

Now there was an action shot of the NSW Grand National Hurdles hanging above the television set, a still painting of a thoroughbred with a ring of roses around it's neck…how in the fuck did this happen? Narcodan?

Before I can really think about all this, in comes Frank the Unbalanced (Guy's been on Aderol, Ritalin, Wellbutrin, Celexa, Paxil, other things I can't spell, for years.), looking tuned up and wired like maybe he decided on introducing a bump or so of speed into his already heavily medicated system…

He rattles off Hello's like machine gun fire, sits in a chair and starts talking to everybody at once, real fast, totally incomprehensible, not a single continuous thread, just, 'Did you see the new Ford F-150? I just got that Remco tap and die set the other day. I can't believe the Mets last night! Garbage! Shit, I gotta put out the recycling tonight. Hey, you guys have any extra beer? I was looking at my back in the mirror last week and pulled out an ingrown hair, fucking thing was 4 inches long! I ordered a pizza yesterday and the damned thing came with anchovies. I think I'm allergic to this new detergent I tried out, I've been itchy all day. I also think there's a rash on my thighs from using a port-a-potty on the job site and...'

And all the time jumping in and out of the chair, dashing to the fridge, grabbing a beer and drinking it in one swig, opening and shutting cabinet doors like he's looking for something but really looking for nothing, spitting a wad of chewing tobacco into the sink, sticking his hand down the back of his pants and scratching at his asshole, also, his chest is vibrating, inhaling large bursts of air and grunting not exhaling, picking cigarette butts from the ashtray, sniffing at them and then dropping them onto the carpet… Frank the Unbalanced, in all his movement and heavy breathing, the way he was bucking around the place…another horse!

It gets to me; the pictures, the Unbalanced, my lack of ejaculation from the night before plus Narcodan makes me cranky after about 10 bumps...I wind up yelling,

"I'm being plagued by these ever fucking, flea-bitten, stirrups and...!"

I weave and march- a drunk with purpose!- into my bedroom. Grab my Frankenstein laptop; things a shell stuffed with some of the finest in stolen, filched, salvaged and traded soundcards, memory modules, hard drive and network adapter, hell, the screen alone took 2 trips to a computer lab with my book bag and a screwdriver, plus all the connecting and reconnecting and reformatting involved... my Frankenstein laptop!

The Giant asks, "What're you doing now?"

"I'm redecorating. I can't deal with all this barnyard, petting zoo, New Jersey stable type..."

"What do you mean?"

"Just look at Frank! You see what all this is doing to him?"

He was galloping through the place, seriously. Just like a kid with one of those broomstick ponies. Huffing and spitting, just missing a saddle and a jockey, Belmont Park, Preakness, The Derby...I see The Blonde inspecting the walls, she nods, and...thank god for an understanding woman...

I start searching eBay by artist name. Look for some of my favorites. Find a Dali reprint of Les Elephants for 5 bucks and order it. (I automatically begin to feel better.) Also a picture of him (Dali) holding an umbrella in a garden and in the upper right hand corner it reads:

'Have no fear of perfection, you'll never reach it.' (Perfect!)

I look up from the screen and see Frank through the window- he's found his way out through the front door somehow- running up and down the street, galloping, foaming, whinnying- loud! (Scared neighbors peeking through curtains and screen doors.)

Then I find a Ralph Steadman reprint of a sketch he did for Hunter Thompson's appearance at the University of Nebraska in

1990, The Blonde approves, says it looks awesome, and I order that one as well.

I start looking for other things, a John Frusciante promo poster from one of his older albums, To Record Only Water, 3 bucks, 11x17, done! A black and white Bukowski print where he's feeding a kitten and looking old! A Misfits banner with a cartoon version of Glen Danzig sticking his tongue out! And then The Blonde gives me inspiration.

"You know, with you being born in Cairo and all, maybe you should get something Egyptian- like maybe a cool papyrus or a statue!"

"You know what, you're right kitten- I've got roots! Bloodline! Lineage and a tan complexion! "

So I start searching for Egyptian art. I find black alabaster cats striking old idol poses, hand woven carpets depicting The Great Pyramids of Giza, key chains inscribed with hieroglyphics, a couple of real nice papyruses with scenes of fishing the Nile, sculptures of Khufu, Tutankhamun, Ramses the 3rd, others and then… item #5385806097 Egyptian Throne / Chair of Sitamun…how I can describe this thing?

"This is an amazingly detailed replica of the famous Egyptian throne of Sitamun. The original seat was made of woven plant fibers and two female heads are set in front of the arms. It is finished in polished bronze and hand painted with a multitude of spectacular golds, reds, blues and greens to give it a colorful and vibrant look. The decoration of the surface of the arms includes four girls carrying trays of gold rings and three images of Bes- a demigod from Babylonia who was imported to Egypt during the 18th dynasty- playing drums and dancing with knives. These hieroglyphs have been painstakingly reproduced by hand and are an exact likeness to those found on the original throne of Sitamun. This is a fabulous example of Egyptian art and would make a welcome addition to any collection. The quality is excellent and it has been finished to a meticulously high standard."

Someone in the UK is selling this thing. The price is listed in pounds, the dimensions in centimeters; I've got a nose full of crushed Narcodan, a stomach rolling with scotch-whiskey and beer, my senses a bit screwy from smoking a joint and my head addled, muddled, crowded and cramped with everything from Steadman to the Derby to…

Frank the Unbalanced has found his way back in through the front door to tell everyone about how whenever he drinks tequila he sleepwalks at night, strips naked, and crawls under his kitchen table…centimeters are how many inches, feet and 35 pounds equals how many dollars, cents, Frank naked under the table? I lit another cigarette and stared off into space; I crawled into a cocoon, I built a spaceship and hopped off the planet, I found a shack in the woods and nailed wooden planks across the door, from the inside...

First I shut my ears to all the noise in the room. Then I removed everyone who was on the couch, in chairs, walking around. Then I pictured myself on a throne, 'The famous Egyptian throne of Sitamun'…I saw myself eating drumsticks the size of a large child's arm. Perfumed Egyptian goddesses wiped my mouth, smiled at me, licked their lips, offered me goblets of wine and wore 3-inch strips of cloth over their breasts. A large scepter adorned with jewels sat close to my right hand. Eunuchs, with curved knives tucked into their waistbands, guarded my chamber…I bid 200 bucks on the thing, jump off the couch, spit the cigarette from my mouth…

"Hail The Great Pharaoh Dempsey!"

"What?"

"The Great Pharaoh Dempsey! Hear me speak!"

"John…"

"You are all my subjects!"

"Well, I'm sure as shit not your subject. I don't see a ring on this finger. Do you?"

"Ring around my ass you impertinent wench!"

"Your ass huh? That's nice John."

"You've been chosen for my kingly harem!"

"I want a harem too!" (The Giant.)

"Quiet! Your Pharaoh is speaking!"

"Blow it out your ass!"

"We must begin erection!"

"Nobody wants to hear about your dick."

"On statues damnit! Something to equal the Sphinx! Cleopatra's needle! The Valley of the Kings! I need monuments!"

"What we need is more beer. Fucking Frank just…"

"Just what? Huh? I didn't do nothing. I say we go get something to eat. Let's barbecue something. Balls! I have to go to the Laundromat and put my clothes in the dryer. Is there a ball game on tonight? Is it supposed to rain this week?"

"Quiet! Your king is addressing you! I demand respect! You, woman, bring me my wine!"

"Screw you."

"And you, eunuch to be…"

"I'm no goddamned eunuch!"

"I said 'to be'!"

"Can't you shut up already?"

"I'm your…"

I woke up Sunday morning, a zombie with an email address:

Subject: eBay Item Won! Egyptian Throne / Chair of Sitamun Trinket Box (Item #5385806097)

Congratulations. You are the winning bidder of item #5385806097 Egyptian Throne / Chair of Sitamun Trinket Box. (I ask myself, trinket box?) You have committed to buy this eBay item from (name withheld).

Click Pay Now to confirm shipping, get total price, and arrange payment through: PayPal; personal check; money order; other.

Trinket box? The Great Pharaoh Dempsey? How much of that shit did I snort last night? Horses? I reread the description. My head's clear enough for me to convert the dimensions:

Height: 18 centimeters is 7 inches (not feet?)

Width: 11 centimeters is 4.5 inches (are you serious?)

Depth: 10 centimeters is 4 inches (what the hell did I do?)

I convert the currency: 50.49 British pounds equal 94.59 American dollars- for a trinket box? What the...!

I receive a second email. This one from the trinket box seller telling me what a fine purchase I made. That the Egyptian Throne / Chair of Sitamun Trinket Box holds earrings, necklaces, a great piece to sit on any woman's makeup table... and all this from pictures, paintings, and posters of horses, dreams of goddesses, drumsticks and eunuch guards, sometimes, especially in the mornings, I get the feeling that I just may be

the brightest

fucking kid in this town.

✿ A FAN, A FEW EMAILS, AND SOME PHOTOS

His email said: I don't like poetry, but I like your poetry.

I replied: That's because I don't type poetry.

He asked: What do you type then?

I told him: I type dirty dreams that I've lived out. I type paranoid fantasies that I've forced into reality. I write busted condoms and broken noses, I write the long dead past into life and fill the pages with zombies. I don't think it can be called poetry.

He answered with: You're right! I can definitely make out the corpses and the pregnancy tests. And yes, you are paranoid. And even though I find myself hoping that you don't actually live this way, another part of me knows that you do. I mean, you've got to be one hell of a good liar to pull it off if you didn't. And I can also understand why you don't think your writing could be called poetry, but that leads me to ask, what would you call it then?

I wrote back: I don't know what to call it. I don't call it anything. When I type it's sessions with a shrink. I'm lying on a couch spilling guts, I'm exorcizing demons, releasing repressed memories, coming to terms with my great I, like I said, I don't know. It's just something I have to do. By the way, how'd you start reading me?

He told me: My girlfriend reads you over at the Expose'd website. She sent me a link saying I should check it out and I did. Then I started typing your name into Google and found some more of your stuff. I'm even thinking about buying one of your books. Which one would you recommend?

I made a recommendation: All of them. Buy 2 or 3 copies of each and help support me. It'll be the greatest act of charity you'll ever pull off. Also, what does your girlfriend look like? Is she cute? And if so, is she kinky? Do you think you could send me a few pictures of her?

His email came back 2 minutes later: Why would you even bring something like that up? I thought you were cool at first, but now I see you're just a dick. I hope nobody buys your books. Go fuck yourself!

I stayed the course: Let's not get off the subject. Buy the books and send me a few pictures. What can it hurt? You'll get something good to read, and your girlfriend will feel sexy. Women like to know that they're lusted after, especially by great artists like myself- I promise, just tell her I asked and you'll make her day.

He replied: I've blocked your email address so don't even bother anymore. And once again, go fuck yourself! Your writing sucks!

Well, maybe I had just lost a fan, but it didn't matter much. I was a great artist, (sure Johnny boy, you just keep telling yourself that) and a new fan would pop up to take his place.

Meanwhile, I thought about his girlfriend. He would tell her what I had said, and she'd get that rush of blood, and sure enough, she'd make plans to take a few pictures of herself when he wasn't around. Then she'd email them to me one day, I'd look at them, and then type up the story of how they came into my possession. Then I'd get the story published- definitely.

He'd read it and confront her. After a while she'd admit it, and the war would start. He'd call her a whore and a tramp. She'd call him a shiftless loser. He would swear revenge on me, and maybe even smack her around a little before heading out to drink with one of his hunting buddies- fantastic.

And then one day in the future I'd feel the edge of a bowie knife pressed against my back while riding the subway, I'd turn around, see some grinning loon, and he'd say 'The greatest act of charity, huh?'

⚭ THE BIG TOP ORGY

the Siamese twins mounted the bearded woman

while the
strong man tongue-kissed
a 65 year old virgin
and the tap-dancing midget
jerked off the Romanian trapeze artist
as the human pretzel
licked his own asshole while the axe juggling clown
opened the mermaid's blouse
and the fire eater
fingered the tattooed lady
as the lion tamer
whipped the singing triplets while the human cannonball
gave the wolf man a reach around
and the snake charmer
sucked off the levitating yogi
as the quick draw artist
ejaculated

prema-
turely
into the mouth of the dancing bear
the two-headed cat
meowed twice
and I sat in the stands
eating popcorn with a hard on, yelling Encore!

Encore!

ℭℛ THE QUICKIE

my sister and brother were in the parking lot, waiting,
the car running and

she got up to lock the door while
I
unrolled the condom

and as I fell into bed
she
pulled off her pants
she got on top-
a few minutes
of warm weather
in winter-

and after
we
got off
she said, "You know I'm taking that last bar of xanax."

෬ Waiting On A Connection With The Music Lover

It was a parked pick-up truck, in a busy parking lot, with heavy rain and time to kill before the pill connection showed up. I rolled cigarettes while the music lover hummed and bobbed his head to the music. The song came to an end- an old-time horn solo, played by an old-time jazz man- and the music lover says,

"The way he plays that thing, it's all emotion, passion, intensity, there's feelings in every breath he blows and each breath is what you'd expect to taste in your mouth kissing some pretty girl, or maybe that metallic blood taste when you get popped if you're off guard and your teeth bust through your lip-skin. Those sounds, they're more physical than anything else. It's a kind of physical music. You know?"

Yeah, I know. This is how he gets when he's been dry for a few days. (The pill connection was 'No dice John, sorry.' for the last week or so.) And this guy in the truck with me, the music lover, he's so used to being slowed down on all that opiate that when the chemical slowness isn't there he zips into hyper speed, almost like he's on coke, talking awfully fast and rambling, with his hands shaking a little, and he reaches out to turn the volume knob on the car stereo, the music gets louder, and he gets louder along with it.

"Listen, just listen to that, that's PHYSICAL music. Right fucking there!"

He stabs his finger at the stereo when he says that last bit and that makes me giggle, the way he stabs his finger in time with his words- 3 words 'Right fucking there!' and 3 stabs.

I listen for a few moments. I don't know much jazz, but I know what's what when it comes to 'physical' music, music that carries something with it, something more than just lyrics and instruments, (like Frusciante, for instance) a force that comes along with the music and messes around with things inside of you, shakes you out of yourself, assaults you on internal levels, and I'm about to answer, to agree with the music lover but before I can get the words out the trumpet begins again and just blares-wails-screams-assaults my insides so much that the mouth opens but words are just no match for what comes out of the speakers- mouth hangs open, hangs open- and when the song comes to an end the music lover turns down the volume and asks,

"See what I mean?"

"Yeah"

"That guy, the way he blows that horn…it's something else. And you know? He had it tough too. I think that's a big part of it. Those sounds he makes, they all stand for something that's happened to him, something he's lived through. Those aren't notes or bars, they're events in his life. He's lived that music and he's blowing his autobiography with that horn."

I get curious.

"What kind of life did he have?"

"A rough one. A ghetto life, with heavy drinking, disappearing-reappearing act, abusive daddy, and mommy in torn slips and bruised face wandering through a one-room apartment just as heavy drinking and abusive as daddy was and him in the middle of it all with them taking turns, him being passed back and forth between wire hangers to belt buckles to hot irons burning the backs of his legs and running to the store with blood in his pants asking for wine on credit."

"That is rough."

"Plus he was queer, and it was the wrong time to be queer, especially black and queer and the guy found no help in any corner and he wound up with the needle."

"Heroin?"

"Yeah, supposedly there was a lot of dope shot through those veins, and a lot of things done to get that dope, things that don't sound so nice in words, but coming out of his horn, those things, while still not exactly sounding nice, sound like something you can listen to, absorb, feel inside you without any of the hang-ups or associations that come from terms like alleyways, dealers, blowjobs. Here, let me queue this particular one up, and I want you to pay real, super close attention to all the details you can hear and tell me just what you get from it."

The volume knob turns again as the song starts up and even at that high volume it's soft at first, sad too, but that's just façade, that's just outside appearances for un-attuned orifices, soon it builds, gets heavier, soon it's all vibrating intestines and mouth hung open…mouth hangs open, hangs open…the body listening and reacting and ears out the window, this isn't something you actually listen to with ears, this is something you feel with cells inside you and they know that there's something in the sound of that horn blowing so hard that the car shakes and your hands move around in your lap like they're dancing to this horn that's blowing straight emotion pulled from the deepest reaches of self…

"All the things that happened to that guy, all the beatings he took from parents and strangers in bars or on the street, the life of running, sleeping in gutters, dreaming demons, all the goodness missed out on, just tragedy, tragedy, tragedy, marked on every day of the calendar, you can hear it, you can feel it, it's enough to make you (tough as nails as you claim to be) want to apologize to his ghost for things that you had no hand in but feel rotten about anyway, makes you with your whole 'I haven't cried since '82' bit want to break down and cry for him right now. What do you think? What did you get?"

"I don't want to cry, you're wrong about that, but I do feel it. It's depressing, sort of, but, uplifting as well. I guess it depends on how you see it, which side of the see-saw you're on. That's what I got."

The music lover takes it in. I've stopped rolling cigarettes because that's just plain impolite in the face of this kind of music. And besides being impolite, it's damned near impossible to do anything but listen and listen with all the parts of you that can listen when something like this is in hearing distance.

I take a deep breath because I feel a little light headed from the horn. Also a little antsy. (I hadn't had anything stronger than beer and weed for a few days and the thought of all those milligrams making their way towards me had me anxious.)

I look around the parking lot, but still no sign of the connection. The music lover nods, I see it out of the corner of my eye, and I can tell that he approves of what I just said, about the see-saw being both sides of that horn.

"Yes! Yes! I saw IT once, both sides of IT, recorded way back with a shaky camera but IT was captured. Black and white footage on a television music channel and at first it sounded like each note was forced air from being kicked in the stomach and ribs, but that's only what you got if you looked at the big ballooning black cheeks and nothing else, that was the depressing part of IT."

"And the uplifting part?"

"That you saw in his eyes, and his lips. He played with his eyes closed and had his lips wrapped around the mouthpiece of that horn like it was his lover. He blew that horn, I thought, anyways, while watching that black and white documentary, knowing he was gay and all, just like he was sucking dick and not some in-need-of-money dick in an alley, but the dick of some long eyelashes lover that was waiting for him backstage or in a hotel.

He blew like he sucked, had to, and I thought that if he sucked like he blew then when you came it wouldn't be semen so much as melody and rhythm bubbling out the head of your dick, that if you took that musical discharge and looked at it under a microscope you wouldn't see that old head and tail shape of sperm, what you'd see would be musical notes all lined up like in a song."

I stopped scanning the parking lot and thought about that for a moment. It was one hell of an analogy, but still,

"I think that that's got to be one of the gayest explanations of technique I've ever heard."

"I don't care. I saw it. You didn't. You were asleep. If you were there or if you had watched that footage with me and had that knowledge that I had, then you wouldn't call it gay, you see,

I'm perceptive, real perceptive when it comes to these kinds of things and behind that man's closed eyes I just knew he was seeing a dark chest, thighs, tear drops of lubricant trembling, about to spill over-"

He stopped in mid-sentence which meant that a white BMW had pulled into the parking lot.

The music lover jumped into the back seat. I counted the money again, making sure I had it split up in such a way that regardless of how many pills the connection was holding I'd be able to do the math and pay him quickly.

The BMW stopped alongside the pickup truck and I turned off the radio. The music lover didn't say a word (guy was too busy salivating), and then the connection was in the passenger seat.

"Sorry about the dry spell, but it's getting harder to fill these scripts."

That meant the price would go up by the next time I met him, and so I bought out his inventory- all of it. He counted the money, and smiled the smile of someone who didn't have any trouble paying the rent. Then the connection was back in his white BMW, and I crushed 500 milligrams with my back teeth. I tossed a pill to the music lover. He caught it in his mouth.

I lit a cigarette and turned the radio back on. The horn started wailing and assaulting us again, and my insides began to shake as I pulled out of the parking lot. And looking in the rearview mirror, I saw the music lover chewing happily, no longer saying anything.

○ॐ To Sit On A Beach In Mexico

To sit on a beach in Mexico drinking
cocktails with The Blonde, the both of us slow
from a mix of...

("Hola. Vende usted vicodin o percocet o oxycontin?"

The same line I've spit out in more than a dozen of these little farmacias since we landed 2 days ago. So far, all I've gotten in reply was 'Arrepentido señor'. Sorry. And the man behind the counter shaking his head. So far, all I've been able to get my hands on is bencoprim, and tramadol. Oh yeah, also a sheet of xanax. But none of that adds up. It isn't what I'm looking for.)

To sit on a beach in Mexico in the morning
drinking cocktails with The Blonde, the both of us
slow from all the rum mixed with muscle relaxers, mood
elevators, and painkillers but still…

(This time it's different. The man behind this particular counter, in this particular farmacia reaches behind him and pulls a sheet of white paper off a shelf. He unfolds the paper and lays it out in front of me. It is written in Spanish, but that's okay. I'm not saying that I can read it. I can't. But I don't need to. All I need is to see certain words. Words like percodan, and adictivo, and I search my brains for matching words, like cuánto.)

To sit on a beach in Mexico
drinking cocktails in the morning with The Blonde,
the both of us
slow from all the rum mixed with muscle relaxers, mood
elevators, and painkillers, real painkillers, the kind that I pay 7 bucks
a pop for at home, but here…

("Quinientos para diez, señor."
I do the math. The guy's talking in pesos, and that's 50 bucks for 10. I nod my head and he puts a small white box on the counter. Then I ask him how many more of those boxes he's got back there and he bends down. When he straightens up I see that he's got 6 of them, that's 300 dollars and I reach for one of my credit cards.)

To sit on a beach in Mexico
drinking
in the sun, and next to me, The Blonde. The both of us
with dilated pupils and tanned legs. The both of us slow from all
the booze and the pills.

There's a waiter
dressed all in white holding a notepad. He's standing in front of
me.

I order 2 pina coladas,
and 2 cans of Sol beer with just
the right accent and as he runs off to get the drinks I think about
perseverance- that's
what I'm made of. John the Perseverant. Sure. Anybody else
would've given up
after being turned down 10 or 12 times, but when something
itches
I usually
scratch 'til it bleeds. The Blonde turns towards me.

"I didn't want two drinks."

"One of them's for me."

"Oh. Do you think we'll be able to take any of those pills home
with us?"

"There probably won't be any left by then."

"You're probably right."

"I'm always right kitty cat."

"Should we get more then?"

"We'll try. Maybe this afternoon I'll catch the bus and head
downtown. See if there are any pharmacies that I might have
missed."

The waiter returns with our drinks. I thank him with my
impeccable
command of the language, and we suck up some more booze.

"Don't forget we have the bullfight at 3:30."

"That's right. Tres y media! Plaza del Toros!"

"You don't have to speak to me in Spanish you know."

"Yes I do."

"No, you really don't."

"I really do though, and you know why, because you're a college girl from Minnesota and you're here on spring break. Yeah. And I'm the handsome Latino you met at the pool bar. Tonight I'll take you out for an authentic Mexican dinner, and afterwards you'll invite me up to your hotel room. I'll wear a sombrero in bed, and you'll straddle me. And the moon will come in through the window and it'll make your shoulders glow. I'll call you mi fantasma hermosa."

"Don't tell me you're already drunk."

"No senorita."

"Then try and act normal."

"I am."

"Shit. I guess you're right."

"I'm always-"

"Yeah, yeah. I know already. Look, I'm gonna try and take a nap. Don't let me burn."

"No problema mi amor."

To sit on a beach in Mexico,
to open a can of Sol at 10 am, to wonder
what happened to reality, without really
being concerned
about it
at all.

ℭℛ THE ROLLING CIRCUS AND A SWEATER

1

Looking up and down the aisles I see them all;

the animals and village idiots,
the curly-haired twats, the lepers, the drunks, the rapists- it's a
full house. I find a seat on this rolling circus and open up 2
things. First it's the tall boy I've got in a brown

paper bag,
and the second is my man Zeta, The Brown
Buffalo.

I keep my head down because if there's any such thing as a
golden rule while on the train it's this: Don't look anybody in the
eyes. Stare at the back of their heads, look at their asses, smell
their perfume, but never make any eye contact. Believe me. All
those soulless freaks and mental defectives, just one look will
turn your hair gray,
will make your dick limp,
will force blood to leak from your ass and run down your
legs…believe me,

I threw out a dozen pair of boxer shorts when I first started
riding this thing,
and I've got too many gray hairs for my age, but my dick
is still working thank
the gods for 6-inch favors. I read a paragraph and take a sip.

2

I should've been better prepared. I read and drink too fast,
finish off Zeta and the tall boy before we even get to Jamaica
station and know
that I'm in trouble.

Why am I in trouble? Because now I've got no armor, no
defense, I can't
bring up my paper-backed shield, I've swallowed all 16 ounces
of my dreams and now
all I can do is look around.

Horror and Trouble.

3

A woman goes into the bathroom
to breastfeed her baby. When she comes out
I see blood
on the child's chin, and a hypnotized
smile
on the woman's face.

2 construction workers take turns
sticking each other's pinkies into their mouths, then finger the
ears of their sleeping friend who wakes up with a giggle.

A group of teenagers heat a paperclip with a Bic lighter,
and brand their initials onto each other's arms and ass cheeks.

Should I go on?

A young girl is screaming into her cell phone, 'Yes, he's the
bastard that gave it to me. I've been scratching at it since last
week and now puss is starting to come out.' Do you believe what
I said before? Horror

and Trouble. I'm not exaggerating. Even the 20 something year
old kid listening to his iPod and staring out the window- don't let
him deceive you, he's
far,
far from normal.

His watch is 24 karat gold with diamonds embedded in its face.
His shoes are the shiniest black leather you'll see outside of a
submission suit. His pants are creased so sharp you could slice
roast beef on his legs. His fingers are manicured. There isn't a
hair out of place on his head. All normal stuff, right? Don't fall
for it. Look closer and you'll see a network of scars running
along his neck. The scars look like the after effect of a run-in

with the howling cat of nine tails. The scars disappear under the
hairline, and down
the neck of his sweater. Just imagine
what he must've done
to deserve it. And also, he's gotta be a maniac. How do I know
this? It's obvious.

The watch and nice clothes are a dead
giveaway. I can tell
that he poses as a young girl in order to talk to children on the
internet. I can tell that he was adopted, and his foster parents
forced hydrogen
peroxide
enemas on him as a small child. And from the looks of his
sweater I can tell that he's got no more

than half a cock in his pants. Believe me. I'm a
real

perceptive guy.

4

I take this all in. I am the recorder. I'm all wide angle lenses and
microphones. A participant? Never. Not I,
says John the irreproachable

from his vantage point of
objectivity.

5

The rolling circus comes to a stop and I run for the doors. I run
through the parking lot. Start my car and pull out of the place
with gravel spraying out from under the tires.
Through
yellow-turning-to-red lights, honking, cursing, switching lanes
without a signal, I'm

escaping.

A Safe Haven.

6

The bedroom with shades drawn, with phone off the hook, with a
sign
on the door,
'Closed for Repairs',
with a bump for the left, and one for the right, I
am a true
man of balance. I wake up fingering Yin,
and spend my nights boxing Yang.
I am the tap dancer with no legs. I am the brain dead
genius
drooling over the apple.

Point and Counterpoint.

Sure. And with this understanding I begin on my
daily quest for balance.

A puff of terror
equals
a puff of smoke, an ounce of horror is an ounce of liquor, a nose
full of fear is a nose
full
of… It's the only way. I reinforce my walls so that none of the
circus animals can come crashing through with their diseases and
infections, with their troubled marriages and teething offspring,
with their nightmares, memories, with their hairy moles and
hyperactive

glands.

7

The next morning is a rerun. Once again the rolling circus.
Once again the animals, the degenerates, the bottom layer of
scum
dredged from the elemental
pool of sub-
humanity closes in around my
less than shiny
soul…

This is my 5-day a week stint in purgatory,
and with each train ride I knock off a little more of the tab,
pay off a little more of the debt that's been accumulated against
me.

Hemmed in the way I am,
I know that I must've pulled something
pretty rotten
in a past life.
I must've killed off some great artist,
raped some sort of saint, disfigured some sort of beauty and
laughed
at the jackal-headed man
at the gates.

8

I chew up a tab of vicodin and take my place in the stands.

7:30 in the morning and 10 milligrams of hydrocodone,

(Remember the walls I was telling you about?
Each milligram is another brick, each milligram fills a gap, plugs a hole
and those walls,
they can never be high enough,
or strong enough.
Every day I've gotta check for cracks, I've gotta make sure that there is no way-
no way whatsoever- for those animals to get inside. I reinforce, I fortify,
I keep my eyes open for stronger building materials (like demerol, oxycontin, fentanyl), because I know
that if anything gets inside,
if any one of those jabbering cunts, jellyfish, cretins, public masturbators, church goers, etc., if even a single one gets in, well,
I am,
no question about it,

screwed.)

behind this wall sits John as close to nirvana
as he
will ever be.

9

I've made it. Penn Station. Last stop.

The rolling circus comes to a halt and all the animals are let loose. They are uneasy with being underground and so they take the stairs on all fours. They snarl, bare teeth, claw at each other, some are in heat, they spray their scents and are mounted in dark corners, some whimper and the urine runs down their hind legs, some battle for the title of alpha, while others are happy with omega, and I
am in the middle of it all. I am caught up in the mass of fur and fear that spills up the stairs. I've got a hundred different scents sprayed on the cuffs of my pants. I'm side stepping around the puddles of piss. I look away as a hyena sinks his teeth into the shoulder
of some fallen

middle-aged
buffalo. And as I'm moving
I feel something- a talon, or a claw, or a flipper of some kind-
poking me in the back.

10

I turn, preparing for an assault by some dancing bear, or the tiger
that jumps through flaming hoops, it could be a walrus or a wolf,
it could be something with tusks or fangs, something hungry, or
horny, or just plain
demented and rabid, foaming at both mouth and crotch, clawing
at whatever's in reach…

You've gotta understand,
there could be
any
thing
behind me.

But I get lucky.
It's one of the more
domesticated animals. Something with a beak, stork legs, a bird
of some sort
wearing a
low cut
shirt.

A (train)ed bird. The beak opens,

"Excuse me."

"Uh, yeah?"

"Just in case you didn't know, there's a hole in your sweater. It's
on the elbow."

(My right elbow gets it the worst. I'm always putting pressure on
it.
No matter what I'm doing- typing, eating, driving, rolling
cigarettes, tickling at my ass with a white feather- no matter what
it is I happen to be doing,
I always seem to be leaning on my right elbow.)

I turn my arm, take a look, and there it is. My right elbow is
sticking out of the hole.
I pull one of the hairs on it.

"Shit. Thanks for letting me know."

"No problem."

"I wish I could repay the favor, but I don't have any seed or fruit
or anything on me."

The bird squawks, flaps her wings
and takes off, showering the crowd
with black and white
droppings.

11

I get to the job.
I put down my bag, put a couple of cigarettes in my pocket,
chew another tab of vicodin, and then get back out onto the
street.

Broadway.

I move along Broadway,
shoulder to shoulder with all the tourists, flashers, perverts and
rub up against you while waiting for the light to change artists.
I'm surrounded by hotdog and pretzel men, the hot nut vendors,
the shish kabob and gyro guys.

There are pale
Asian girls
shouldering Hello Kitty book bags and snapping pictures and
they've all got the bird flu– I'm positive of it!

There are skinny
black
homosexual types with mohawks wearing sarongs, sandals, and
mesh t-shirts, an eruption of puss-filled
blisters around their lips. I get jostled by pickpockets, bumped by
chubby Spanish chicks, sized up by hoodlums, and the pretty
girls
who aren't wearing bras
give me dirty looks as I drool onto my shoes.

I eventually get to a clothing store.

I spend about 7 minutes watching a salesperson undress a mannequin.
Then I wander over into the women's section to look at the panties, touching a couple,
like I'm examining the fabric. Then I remember what I came in here for.

The sweater.

I find one in the back of the men's section. On sale. Padded elbows. Perfect.
I also see a shirt that I like. The color's a little weird, but I figure why not.
I find my size and get in the dressing room.

The shirt fits pretty well and I decide to buy it. Then I try on the sweater.
That also fits well. Plus it's got those padded elbows. It's a nice sweater. It makes me look like a clean-cut kid, and as I'm posing in the mirror- resting my chin on my hand, pretending to hail a cab, tilting my head to the side, cocking an eyebrow and smiling- I realize that I've seen this sweater someplace before. It's familiar. I start thinking about it, and after a few minutes it hits me. That kid on the train! The maniac! The one with all those scars on his neck and the iPod and the enemas! The one that's only got
half a...

I hold my breath while I undo my belt, unbutton, un-zipper, drop my pants and boxers...

It's still there. My cycloptic buddy and confidant. My copilot.
The spelunker.
The interior
decorator.

I contemplate masturbating, just to make sure that everything still works. An examination more than anything else. Something to give me piece of mind, but I don't do it.

(Regardless
of what you may think about me,
I am able to exercise self-restraint.

Sometimes anyway.) I get dressed quickly and jump out of the
fitting room. There's a skirt that looks as if it's been tried on
hanging over the door of one of the other rooms.
I grab it, turn it inside out, take a whiff, and then drop it on the
floor.
It smelled somewhat like onions.

12

I put on my nice new shirt and work my way through the day.
I pop vicodin and smoke cigarettes.
I delete my coworker's emails without responding.
All calls go to voice mail. I play Scrabble and type dirty stories
and somehow
I make it.

Quitting Time.

As I close in on Penn Station the fear starts. And it isn't anything
as simple as paranoia. Believe me.
I only wish that was the case.

I'm the voice of experience. I can tell what to expect.
I'll get on the rolling circus
and all the animals will be waiting for me. It will be an orgy of
harassment and molestation. I will be stuck with no way out,
trapped while the show goes on all around me.

I've done this so many times
that I can even tell you what the lineup will be
without having to look at a program.

Some randy bastard wearing a lime green button down
and white pants will dump a bottle of water on his lap.
He'll walk up and down the car displaying the outline of his cock
and winking like some kind of deranged nymphomaniac.

A yeast infected beast will settle down next to me,
and she'll spend 20 minutes digging at her crotch with red claws.
Some mongoloid child will crawl under the seats and dry hump

my work shoes. And I will go mad
one act
at a time. Once the show ends
I'll be a loon. I'll think crazy things. I'll say to myself,

'John, if by some chance, when you get off this train you notice
a prostitute, and if by some chance she happens to be French,
then you must go home and get your pocket knife. You must
hold it against her throat while burning her with cigarettes for 14
hours.

Only then will the both of you be saved. She will thank you, and
open her arms to you, and as the sun comes up she will make
you a breakfast of crepes and strong coffee.'

Repulsive thoughts,
things that I would never think of in any other environment- but
I'm also resigned to it. I find my place in the stands and the
conductor comes by. I go to show him my ticket
and he waves it aside.

"No entrance fee for the performers."

"What?"

"Why the hell would you pay to see your own act?"

"My act?"

"That's right, 5 minutes to show time. You better get in
costume."

And as he walks away I look myself over. My nice new shirt,
yup, lime green.
I'm wearing white pants.
And as the lights are dimmed, I pull out a bottle of water from
my book bag,
and listen
for my cue.

❦ A Not So Strong Constitution

a small glimpse of his mortality
and the young man crumbles

we find him kneeling
on the tiles
poking at the blood clots in the toilet

with a short length
of rolled cardboard

❦ The Eaters Of Chocolate

They were waiting on the subway platform. It was 2 of them. Young, about 25 years old, in the middle of July, and I stood 10 feet away.

I was pretending to be a tape recorder, while thinking what kind of a story it would make. (After listening for a few minutes I decided to flip the tape. Side A was a poem about a girl in high heels, walking through soup suds in Manhattan, her footprints evaporating behind her. The Mexican kid sweeping down the sidewalk watched the sway of her ass for a moment, then whispered puta.) The tape was flipped, and I hit record.

"I just couldn't help it."

"Cravings!"

"Oh my god. I wound up in that little French place just off St. Marks."

"That place is so evil."

"It is the devil. But it was just so hot in the apartment. And all I could think about was that mousse they make."

"Oooh."

"I said to hell with my figure. Summer's almost over anyway."

"That's so true."

"Let me tell you, as evil as that place is, their mousse is heaven."

"Heaven!"

"And it was just a tad extra bit of heaven last night, in all that heat. I just sat there all by myself, just eating and smiling."

"That's so sad. You shouldn't have been there alone."

"Oh, I didn't mind. Besides, the mousse kept me company. It was so smooth and thick. It was so rich. It reminded of the first time I took Phillipe in my mouth. Do you remember Phillipe?"

"How could I forget him? He was an obsidian angel. He had skin like an eggplant. His eyes were oval pools of spilt oil."

"And his palms. They were so pink! I remember I would kiss them and think of almost-ripe strawberries."

"He really was sweet."

"Just like the mousse. It reminded me so much of him. Too much of him. I almost went off in my pants."

"You dog!"

"In heat!"

"Yeee! You know what else is good. Those chocolate covered truffles they sell at that bakery in Astoria. The ones they keep in the fridge and you have to ask for them."

"Don't even get me started. It's always chocolate. Chocolate cake, chocolate ice-cream, chocolate pudding, last night, the chocolate mousse- and you know what?"

"What?"

"I blame it all on black men."

"Oh, baloney."

"I do! Being with black men has turned me into such a little piggy for chocolate."

He looked down at his feet, grinning, and shaking his head, thinking about the correlation. Then he looked back up, the grin even wider.

"I can't even begin to think of a reply to that."

"It's just that I can't say no to anything with chocolate in it."

"Well, it's pretty hard saying no to something that's so yummy."

"I know, but I really do need some kind of self control. Just a little bit even."

"Ah, self control's overrated. I say enjoy yourself."

"But my waist."

"Who cares about your waist? I know I don't."

"Um, yeah, but I do."

"You're so not fat."

"Then why am I getting these little love handles?"

"Where?"

"Well," He pulls his shirt up to just below his chest, and turns to the side, grabbing at the beginnings of a spare tire (And I caught a shot of shiny, light blue cloth at the waist line, with a patterned overlay of black lace.

It reminded me of The Blonde, (my long-haired, understanding, and heavy breathing when we kiss) girlfriend-which was weird.),

"Over here. And here. And- Hey! Quit it!"

(Ah…the ability to appreciate
these
small glimpses
of an alien
life.)

On the pretense of checking the subway route they're standing next to I move a few feet closer. That's just how I am. If I'm recording, I make sure to get everything. I don't want half-sentences, or garbled words that I have to reconstruct with imagination- I want it just as it was. I want all the nuances and noises. I want the tones, the turns in conversation, the squeals, the giggles...

(I'm a social connoisseur.

I'm the biggest big-game hunter there is, shooting Life in the wild, and mounting the trophy heads on a computer screen.

I'm an avid collector of things, like people and situations that I stumble upon, don't fully understand, and the tape recorder/camera part of me comes out.)

They were having a tickle fight. It lasted for about a minute, and left them out of breath, a little sweaty, panting, and standing a few feet away from each other, hands on their hips. Then the subway came. The uptown E.

They got on and stood in the middle of the car. I leaned against the door and started taking pictures. (I know I keep cutting in, but I'm tweaked out typing in the afternoon and I don't want you to get the wrong idea. I don't own a camera; I just pretend to take pictures. Or better yet, sometimes I just pretend that I'm a camera. That's it. If I squint it's the same as hitting a button marked zoom. I'm Nicky Nikon! Milty Minolta! Sure. And when I need to get the pictures developed I go into the darkroom, which is just me closing my eyes while typing. Perfect.)

They were tall, wearing t-shirts, jeans, and sandals. One of them had holes in his jeans, around the knees and back pocket. The other guy's t-shirt said 'Proud' across the front, with rhinestones outlining multi-colored letters. They were clean shaven, their finger and toe nails clipped, their hair brushed, styled, highlights for one, and wavy, meticulously brushed curls for the other. The one with the highlights and the spare tire had a few raised patches of red chafe around his lips, like he was coming off an outbreak.

"I don't know, I didn't feel any love handles."

"Well, they're still there. I saw them this morning when I was getting dressed."

"Oh, you were probably just feeling guilty from the mousse."

"Maybe."

"So did you decide what you want to do tonight?"

"Well, I was going to go down to Havana's for drinks, but I'm just so sick of that crowd. All they ever do is bitch and hiss at each other. All they ever do is get into these catty little arguments."

"Yeah, and even worse, they have absolutely no sense of style. Come on. Early 90's I'm-finally-out fag scene- no thank you."

"And, well, You Know Who is coming home from school this weekend, so I guess I should clean up the apartment."

"Don't tell me you're still seeing her."

"Uh. I know, I know."

"But I thought you said that you were done with that. No more trying to get back into the womb."

"I am… I'm not. But. I just don't know what to do. She's like my big sis now. I call her Sissy, and everything… We eat sorbet and watch old musicals on AMC."

"Yeah, but she still makes you have sex with her. You drink that cheap Zinfandel and then you…"

He couldn't finish the sentence. He shook his head, then turned, and started staring through the subway window. The other one looked down at the floor, sulking.

14th Street. The subway came to a stop. The doors opened and a few people got on at either end of the car. Then the doors closed. The one looking out the window turned to the one looking at the floor. He felt the stare, and after a few seconds he looked up, his face composed, his Naughtily Angelic look; innocent, yet with a small, mischievous smile that not a boy in the world could deny.

The other one couldn't help himself. He smiled too. (I think that I might've even smiled. That's just how I am.)

"Well, I do use condoms you know."

"I really hope so, Waltz."

"Oooh. You. You. I always love it when you call me that. Waltz. Say it again."

"Waltz. Waltz. Waltz!"

"It makes me feel like something graceful."

"You are. That's why I call you that, Waltz, you're the waltz done just right with coattails and gowns and the whole scene with a big band playing soft. Waltz. Just like in those old musicals."

"Oh."

"Besides, Walter is just so, it's so, utilitarian. You know? It doesn't fit you at all."

"Because I'm a swan?"

"A beautiful swan, with soft white feathers and a long beak and-"

The door connecting the subway cars slid open and a young girl came through it. She was only semi-pretty, but the way she was built and dressed made up for it. I took a picture of pear-shaped breasts, their round tops coming out of a low-cut white tank-top. Unfettered, unconfined, free to roam without a bra, the nipples were erect, bulging brown beneath the loosely-stitched, almost see-through white fabric.

Then I took a picture of her legs. They were tanned, and dripped like double-malt, 18-year-old and legal scotch-whiskey from a pair of pink, terrycloth shorts that barely reached the beginning of her thighs. The shorts sat low on her hips, and as she walked towards me I snapped a picture of intoxicating hip bones. After she passed, I got a shot of her ass crack, surrounded by toned muscle. I also got a shot of a single long, curly hair that sprouted out from beneath the back of her shorts and snaked towards her tailbone. 23rd street and I had stopped being a camera. I had turned back into a tape recorder.

"Uh, Gregory, do you see what just walked in?"

"Don't do it Waltz. There's no need."

"But do you see what she's wearing?"

"Yes. I do. And I'm just as disgusted as you are, but still, it's a free country. Well, parts of it anyway, like Vermont, and she's got a right to wear whatever she wants."

"But, it just gets to me. So bad sometimes! If she can show off her ass, then why the hell can't I?"

"Who says you can't? Go ahead. Shake it. Show her that you've got it just as much as she does. Show us all. C'mon, Waltz."

"Greg. Don't tempt me."

"Let's see."

"I'll do it."

"Ah. You're all bubblegum and talk. You wouldn't dare."

"Oh yeah?"

They stared at each other. The subway was slowing down. 34th street. Penn Station. My stop.

I had a train to catch, but, the whole dedicated artist thing, the whole obsessive, compulsive, 'John you must get this story. You absolutely have to get this story. You'd be an idiot not to see it through till the...' The train empties out onto the platform.

Everyone gets off at Penn except for our 2 main characters, the guys I've been recording. And myself. And the girl with the ass crack. Also some other people. The rest of the commuters spilled out of the doors, and down the stairs, fluid, a flock of birds migrating, a herd of deer on the move, a large school of salmon swimming upstream, all the animals you've ever heard of and some that are simply beyond imagination... Then the doors closed.

Greg and Waltz continued staring at each other. Waltz smiled. The subway started moving towards 42nd.

And then Waltz had his belt loosened. He turned, pointed his ass at Greg, and lowered his pants about an inch or so. Beneath the pants he was wearing a pair of blue women's underwear. (And that's why I connected it earlier. The Blonde. She's got a very similar pair, and immediately, I made plans to throw them out once I got home.) Also, there was glitter on his ass cheeks. He started shaking his ass. Greg suddenly looked as if he hadn't eaten in days.

"Oh! You whore!"

42nd street. Waltz pulled his pants up and Greg wiped at his mouth.

"You're such a little tease."

"No, it's just that I've got a right to wear whatever I want, however I want. If she can do it, well then I can too."

"You're so right."

"Of course I am. And now I'm going to go and pull her hair."

"Don't you dare do that!"

"Well, can I at least call her a slut?"

"No!"

"Just a little slut?"

"Waltz! Behave yourself. If you're good, then I'll take you for a milkshake."

"Mmmm. A chocolate milkshake?"

"What else? There's this place in midtown, they make them so thick it's impossible to suck through the straw."

"Not for me it isn't."

We were coming up on 50th street. The subway slowing down, Waltz taunting, Greg hungry, and I was running out of both tape and film. I wouldn't be able to remember too much more. At least not with clarity, details would get lost. And definitely not with continuity, the life of the thing itself would become unstable, shaky as the subway where all this is taking place and that's the problem with pretending. You can only take it so far before the reality of a bigger picture sets in.

You can only imagine so much, only in so many directions, before you bang into something that's way more concrete. (And I think that's part of the reason I followed these guys. They knew what they were, and they were as concrete with it and themselves as anything built by man.) The subway came to a stop and I recorded the last bit:

They stood against the subway doors, waiting to be let out. Greg stared at Waltz, who continued to smile, and looked at his reflection in the plastic paneling of the subway doors. He kept making little changes to his face, shifting his lips, slitting his eyes, turning so that his chin was more pronounced.

"You know what? Instead of Waltz I'm going to start calling you Dyson, like the vacuum cleaner."

"Uh-uh. It sounds too German. No. The only name I'll ever answer to is Waltz. Waltz forever!"

"Then come on, Waltz, let's get off this train and go for a milkshake."

"Ah, Greg, what would I ever do without you?"

"You'd shrivel up like a flower with no water."

"I'd simply die."

"And then I'd have no one to eat truffles or drink milkshakes with. I'd be the loneliest boy in all of Manhattan."

"Oh!"

"In all the world even!"

"Yeah."

The subway doors slid open, 50th street, and I had missed my train. But I did have a story. It felt good. It always feels good. No matter how bad the story might turn out, that first second, right after you get it, when you know you've got it, completely, 100%, no question about it, it's all there and pretty soon you'll have it mounted like a trophy head, it'll be up on that computer screen and it'll be just as it was, just as you saw and heard it, just the way you recorded it running in the wild before aiming and firing... definitely.

Our main characters made their way above ground, and presumably, went for chocolate milkshakes. I made my way over to the platform marked 'Downtown', and waited for the subway to come.

℞ THAT'S IT. SURE.

You see your name, your words, and you think
to yourself
that's it. Sure. That's me up there. And even if people don't see
it yet,
I'm up there with the big guys. I'm sitting around with giants,
and we're all drinking classy booze,
and maybe even
trading fishing stories. Sure.

And when I finally give it up,
there will be strangers at my funeral. Also camera men. And
farm girls
from the mid-west
will cry over me
even though
they've never
seen my face. Men in prison cells will go into mourning. And the
ones who knew me
will all say, 'He was too much. He was too big. He was too wild
to stay locked up
in the big zoo.' Sure.

But while I'm here, looking around, weighing everybody else,
all those
other guys,
the ones with degrees, success, book signings, the ones with well

thought out hearts,
easy nights where nothing chases them, the ones with all those
nice
palatable
lines
just bursting from their fingertips...I know that they have neither
the grace
nor the guts
to wipe at my ass.

⌘ SIMPLE THINGS

I like simple things like buttons and zippers and hooks
being undone
simple things like
my headboard
banging against the wall
simple things like
your hair in my mouth
and the way you smoke a cigarette
while cursing, and looking around the room
for your shirt.

⌘ PARANOID?

On the train I hear someone talking, 'I used lots of olive oil and
garlic.' and that's nothing
to be afraid of. I open my book, a collection of essays by Simic,
and right away, guess what, hello,
(she'll call it paranoia) word for word, the first 2 sentences I
read, 'She cooked southern Italian dishes. Lots of olive oil and
garlic.' I look at the someone that was talking; an assassin. No
question about it, an assassin, but he's slipped up and I caught it,
we lock eyes,
and then I get up (walking away

I hear him trying to cover up the mistake, 'Kid must not like
Italian food.' Too late,
too late would be killer, you
will not coax this kitten out from under the couch with
that
kind of milk.) and so I move to the next car.

"It's just a mix of paranoia and coincidence." Says The Blonde.

"Bullshit."

"No one's trying to kill you."

"Maybe not consciously. But nonetheless, some thing or body's
working on it. I can tell."

"You're paranoid."

"It's called self-preservation."

"It coincidence! Just coincidence! So what if he said olive oil
and garlic, there's nothing weird or threatening about that. Just
coincidence."

Then standing on the subway platform. It's empty except for the
guy that
just has to-
absolutely has to-
regardless of all the open space he simply must stand next to me.
He's
scratching a lottery ticket with his thumbnail,
he's not even looking at it, he's
waiting for the right moment, the moment that the downtown E
rounds the bend,
so he can reach out and send Johnny
head over heels onto the tracks. I hear the E, the guy stops
scratching,
and as he steps towards me
I turn on my heel (scared
but still fluid, John
you're a ballerina at her first recital-
sure), I push through the crowd,
go back through the turnstile,
and it looks like

I'm
walking to work.

"Coincidence, huh? That's a term used by people with untrained eyes and ears."

"You're delusional!"

"No, I'm just attuned."

"Attuned? Attuned to what?"

"All manner of things."

"More like all manner of nothing."

"Would you call instinct nothing? How about premonition? All nothing- right? And what about the other day when you called me right before you went in the shower?"

"What about it?"

"As soon as I hung up a woman on TV said she was going to beat her cat."

"So?"

"So? You were going in the shower to masturbate."

"I was not!"

Then on the street, I don't see them
but I know that they're there. 2 guys.
Heavyset, slicked back hair, wearing trench coats, walking
behind me and any minute they'll come up
on either side of me, grab me by the elbows as a black van
pulls up
and the sliding door
slides open, 'Let's go for a ride.' I
find myself running up the block. I turn a corner. There's
an old woman feeding bread to pigeons, and as I pass her
I see something shiny along with the bread in her hand, either
a throwing knife or a silver bracelet, out of breath, I duck behind
a parked car
and continue running up the block- everybody's after me. I know
it.

My car was towed
so that they could trap me in the impound yard
and release attack dogs.
The delivery boy poisoned my beef and broccoli because I
screwed his girlfriend
12 years ago
and now she calls out my name in her sleep while
thrusting out
at the hips. (and what's weird is 2 nights back, in bed, half
asleep, I heard moaning,
felt hot breath against my face, and then an
unexplainable
wetness on my balls- an
astral projection of cunt!) I just know it. A thousand assassins
and one target. A thousand killers
and they all want
my jizz,
my blood,
and my brains
to pretty up
the sidewalks and their mattresses with. A 30 block dash to the
job, I walk in the place, wondering
how long I can keep it up, when will it be my turn to slip, drop
my guard,
and get that string around my toe,

"You're losing it. If you said something like that to a psychiatrist
they'd lock you up."

"I don't know, there was definitely a strange wetness around my
balls, and it wasn't sweat, it was discharge. Astral discharge."

"I'm not listening to this anymore."

"But aren't you worried? Or jealous even?"

"Worried about what?"

"My death!"

"You aren't dying anytime soon."

"And you're not jealous?"

"Of your wet dream? Why would that make me jealous?"

"It wasn't a wet dream. It was some sort of cosmic orgasm. Or maybe a succubus!"

"You were probably just jerking off in your sleep."

And that's possible, but still,

"So you've been watching me sleep, huh?"

"I'm not listening anymore."

"You have!"

"Uh! That's enough. There are no assassins coming after you, no succubus in your bed, and I definitely, definitely don't watch you sleep. I can barely stay in the same room with you when you're sleeping."

"Something tells me you're lying."

"Okay honey, I'm lying, now please, let's just drop it."

And she sits there, shaking her head

while I watch her

out of the corner of my eye.

✂ I COULD'VE BEEN

the best feather-weight boxer that's ever stepped into the ring

knocking out

wiry Mexicans and

sinuous

black dudes

‷ GREAT MOMENTS

there are certain moments,
undeniably great moments, perhaps the best
that time has in store for you, the wind screaming through an
open
car window,
a beautiful girl in the passenger seat
without any panties on, you're both laughing at 70
miles an hour down the highway with
no traffic,
just good music, and a pocketful of cash,
on your way
to pick up 50 vicodin.

‷ IMAGINE THAT

From now on I will be writing under Victoria Hardlace
so look for
my erotic,
rhyming poetry under the Love section in anthologies,
magazines
and websites, also

I will begin taking yoga classes, meditating, eating healthy,
cutting back on
my drinking,
smoking,
I will stop taking pills that have not been prescribed to me,
I will not dream about poppy fields where teams
of beautiful women
work the fields- my fields- while I watch over them from some
front porch,
puffing cigars, and occasionally
sticking my fingers inside some teeny opiate addict, instead I
will exercise,

ride my bicycle,
go running in the mornings, lift weights
3 times
a week and think nice,
rational,
good-natured, optimistic thoughts, I will begin studying for
graduate school

entrance exams, and saving up
to buy my first home, I will also get married,
impregnate The Blonde and rub her belly each night before we
fall asleep
spooning, I will see a doctor about the wart on my index finger, I
will go to the dentist

to have
my rotten teeth removed and implants
put in to fill the gaps, I will no longer wear clothes with cigarette
burns, blood stains,
holes or hardened semen
by the zipper, I will not masturbate as if it were an essential act
of staying alive, I

will control my urges,
impulses, my temper, I will not call children on the street
mongoloid bastards,
I will not refer to people by crude names like
Big Titted Becky,
Jimmy the Jizz Junky,
or Long Island Linzy with the Long-Lipped Pussy (her labia
measure 6 inches
a piece
when stretched), I will stop spitting on handrails and door
handles, never again will I piss in the public

drinking fountain at the park or in the soap
dispensers of restrooms, I will love
my fellow man and woman and all of their children and respect
their right to breathe just
as much as my own, I will attend weddings, birthday parties,
celebrate holidays

around
the fireplace and sign my name to presents with a smiley face
underneath, I will send flowers
to my mother on random days, I will send my father a handwritten letter

telling him he is the strongest man I have ever known, I will
recognize the value of my sister's kindness, and learn how to
accept my
younger brother's compliments (he knows all about me), I will
answer the phone when people call me and I will have long
conversations and share feelings, ask how their day was,
remember the names
of their dogs and
coworkers- coworkers!- from now on I will be friendly with all
of my coworkers, I

will not call them vampiric cocksuckers,
I will not say they have condom-coffee-blood breath, instead

I will leave notes of congratulations in their mailboxes when
they are promoted,
I will order teddy bears for the whole fucking office on
Valentine's Day,
and write a personal note for each one of my
delightful
teammates
on a heart-shaped
card, I will no longer talk down to people, no more
condescension, not from sweet-as-pie,

accommodating, helpful-at-all-times John,

I will no longer curse and yell at the television or the radio, in
fact,

I will no longer yell or curse at all, I will cultivate my speaking
voice and I will clean up
my vocabulary,
removing terms from the inventory such as cunt-eye, cum-
mouth, cock-toe, I
will not scream "God's ever-fucking balls!" when I become

impatient or frustrated,
or punch my alarm clock in the mornings,
or hit the button marked 'Door Close' on elevators when I see people
running
to get in the car with me, I will help the blind cross through
traffic, I will help the elderly

do their grocery shopping, and I will sign up
to become a mentor to some inner-city
youth, I will organize relief funds
for victims
of natural disasters, I will help chaperone high school dances and
make sure that nobody
doses the punch
with liquid acid,

I will not allow strange legs and asses to lead me down strange
streets, I will no longer
objectify the opposite sex, or shy away from handshakes, hugs,
kisses hello and good bye, I will
learn to appreciate human contact on a level
outside of

bodily discharges and fluid
exchanges, I will shovel my neighbor's driveways when it
snows, and rake their lawns
in the fall, from now on

I will not search for an everyday escape hatch, or a way out,
instead, I will integrate myself with the world (the whole
world!), all of you mixed with all of me, I will take myself out
of the center of the universe and hand space
over to somebody else, I will do all of these things, sure, just
wait, you'll see, one day, I'll pull it all off and
you'll never hear from me

again.

෪ WEST 3RD SYMMETRY

The young Spanish busboy with the ponytail
wears his white
busboy's outfit
and a pair
of rubber gloves.

He dumps a bucket of
soapy water
onto the sidewalk
in front of the restaurant and then he scrubs,
working to remove the chewing gum and bird
shit
stains

Then a young woman
wobbling, uncomfortable
in
high heels
walks through the suds.

The busboy curses under his breath
in Spanish
at her back, while
reaching for a hose.

The young woman continues walking
and with each step
the imprint of her shoes
is left
on the sidewalk (heel-toe). She turns a corner,
the footsteps slowly
evaporating behind her, just another
pretty
ghost on the hustle.

And walking to work I see this
and think to myself,

poetry,
so much
goddamned poetry
in this city
that it almost balances out the madness

of its citizens.

◘ CORRESPONDENCE (A BUILDING BLOCK)

I unlocked the door of my apartment. I walked in. I wasn't
feeling well. Too much shit on my mind. Too much bad luck.
Too much rejection. Too much of everything and it was
weighing me down. I noticed a stack of mail. I saw my name on
one of the envelopes.

Dear Mr. Dempsey,

On August 24th, The St. Louis Council for Arts and
Letters will open our latest exhibit to the public, 'A
Most Dangerous Profession'. As you know, from the
inclusion of your work, this exhibit will be a display of
poetry and short stories, all of them handwritten, by the
most progressive writers of our time. We are
reaching out to you in the hopes that you will deliver a
short speech during the opening ceremony, as an
introduction to the work on display. All traveling and
hotel fees will be covered by the St. Louis Council, and
a speaking-fee of $3,000 is offered as compensation. If
you are interested in...

Who is this Council? What is St. Louis? Was someone
dreaming tsunami, thunderbolts, earthquakes, mountains
crashing up through the earth when some far-off editor opened a
mailbox in the morning? (They were.) How many pills do you
think I can get for $3,000? (Enough.) How many days would I
call in sick to the job? (A lot.) I was starting to remember, and
with memory came a better feeling, a lighter feeling than what
I'd been carrying around.

Then I saw another letter. It was from Nebraska. It looked like a woman's writing.

> John! Johnny! Mr. Dempsey! It's Me! You don't know Me! I've written this letter 15 times! I tried being intellectual, well-read, then college-girl kittenish, coy, flirtatious, then I read something, felt something, and remembered what this letter was all about- YOU! What YOU did- do to me. I read a poem, sweat breaks out across my tits, I start squirming, I get scared that when I stand up a puddle will be there. It's too much! I am saving money to come to New York. I want to meet you. I want to ask you questions. There is a long leather string tied around my waist, and at the end of it is an empty vial from a perfume sample. I made it after I read *Bailing*...

I pictured a lanky, countrified cunt with strong legs from riding horses. She had dirty blonde hair, blue eyes, buck teeth, scars on her forearms, freckles, hog-tying knowledge, melon-shaped breasts with wide, bumpy nipples, the ability to suck half-dried cement through a cigarette filter... I then decided that if she ever came to New York I would send her home with a mouth-full of inspiration. Also that vial. It would be just like in that Roald Dahl book.

Then I saw that there was another letter, and I started to feel even better, a little lighter.

> Mr. John Dempsey. Hello. I am writing to you from Vermont. I live here, in a commune, with a bunch of people who've got the right ideas. We listen to the Misfits and go snowboarding and stick-up pharmacies. We grow tobacco, tomatoes, cucumbers, lettuce, pot, poppy, and mushrooms. We are in the process of buying 2 cows and 2 goats. We've all read your books. We're building our own escape. Can you help? The address is...

A fanatic. Definitely. And I liked the sound of him. He seemed like he had some of the right ideas. The Misfits are great.

I've often dreamed of growing tobacco. And as for escape, well...

It was turning out to be a good day after all. All the shit and dirt that had been piling up on me from things like the job, the life, the subway hustle, the endless jabbering of dead words, the nodding of empty heads, the waiting in line for my spot in some concentration camp, the endless want of more and more, the constant movement towards no end, the constant dreaming, the constant let-down, the double-cross pulled at first breath, the 'Bad News Johnny Boy' splattered on every fucking newspaper, all that shit, and all that dirt that makes up the waking world, it starts flaking off, it all just starts falling off to the side and I walk away from it all...

*

There was no reason for it. No reason for the depression, the self-loathing. No reason to think I was going nowhere, producing nothing, being nobody. I was holding the proof! These people actually care! They took time out of their lives to contact me, to offer me things, to show that they are out there and reading, to let me know that I'm not alone...and it felt good.

*

I start to realize that I have everything in front of me. It's all just there! Waiting for me to grab hold of it! Whatever I want! Endless medication! A Brewery! 3 whorehouses! A grant from the Guggenheim! A ski-house on the west coast! An index finger without a wart on it! Anything I want! I can have it all! I can conquer anything! No matter what astronaut from the past landed before me! No matter what flag with what name this territory is now the property of John Dempsey, master of all man and beast, ravisher of all pink and apricot fragrant trap, writer of all words, pusher of all buttons with a finger in each hole! Yes!

And who cares if I'm the one who wrote all these letters. What does it matter that I'm the one who took out envelopes, thought all these words, took on all the personalities, got my address off a driver's license. So what if I wrote, sealed, stamped and mailed...it doesn't take any of the value away. The action itself means nothing; it's the reasoning behind the action that counts-the big 'Why?'

'Okay. So, why'd you do it Johnny?'

Because I'm a builder. I'm a creator. This is what I do. These are all parts of the big picture. The letters, the words, the personalities behind them, they have now become real to me. I will speak at the opening ceremony! I will send a cowgirl home with a memorable taste in her mouth! I will drive to Vermont, become part of the commune, live off the fat of the land and knock over pharmacies just like in that movie with Matt Dillon! Definitely!

*

Don't you see how good I feel right now? Do you understand why I would do these things? Why I would believe and run with these things? Wouldn't you do the same if you were me? (And if you've answered in the negative then you're lying. Or you're a dope. You're also blind and you've got no idea how to dream.) Just think about it for a minute. What else could I possibly do? Faced with a world that I don't like, and can't change, what can I do? If I find myself trapped in an unappreciative, insensitive, blood hungry, pulled-apart-at-the-seams kind of a world with no clearly marked exits what the hell
can I
possibly do?

*

'Uh…The only thing you can do?'

That's right! A stuffed bear for the mark that's hit the bulls-eye!

I build.

*

I've created my own world. I've made all the buildings the shapes that I like- fuck gravity, stress points, logical architecture, my home will be an upside down pyramid and all the staircases will be like M.C. Escher drawings.

This world is populated only by readers throwing flowers, blowing kisses, and offering up their supple daughters in the hopes that I'll pluck a curly lock of pubic hair from under their Sunday dresses.

All the laws will be laws that I can actually understand. Legal suicide! Medication without prescription! Victimless crimes will go unpunished, the clouds will pour mescaline every other Wednesday, and a bullet to the back of the head for every cocksucker talking loudly on a cell phone when I'm on the train.

Monetary system out the window! Instead of a rent check I will mail my landlady a short story. Instead of paying credit card bills I will send a poem to American Express, tap dance in front of the Visa building, play guitar for a MasterCard representative and they will all wipe out my debt! If I paint a picture I can trade it in for a new car! If I take a photo then I can go to the mall and exchange it for new clothes!

Yes! More! Biologic judgments will be reversed. Cigarettes will promote health! The more alcohol I drink the more in-tune my body will become! Smoking pot will strengthen the memory! Promiscuous, unprotected, alleyway sex with strangers will have no viral or social repercussions! And I plan to push it further! Build! Create! Yes!

*

This is what I do. It is the only thing that I can do. If it weren't for my world, for my people, my dreams, I'd have called it quits a long time back. If it weren't for all my characters and words I'd be a hopeless head case. I'd be one of those guys sitting in the corner of some padded room, in some out of the way facility, rocking back and forth with my arms tied around my back and shit stains on the seat of my pants. The sun would be out of the question. The heart would've never been born. The soul would've jumped out in a hiccup, dissipated, and the fingers turned to concrete...

*

But instead of all of that, I have this; my little homemade world. A world built on words, brushstrokes, rhythms, photographs, dreams…and there's a feeling of belonging that I've never had in all my time stumbling around mother earth.

*

Now you try it! Don't forget any of the details! Make your world complete. Write, paint, photograph, beat at the drums and act your world into existence. Cover all bases. Classifications out the window! Don't identify yourself as a writer, painter, photographer, musician, actor, dancer! No! You are a Creator! All classifications are good for is to confine you to medium! Break out of that!

Dream and build your way out of it! Sculpt your way out of it! Do it all! Create until you find yourself on a globe that spins at just the right speed for you. Create until you're surrounded by lovers and admirers. Create until the heavens look down at you with jealousy, and if that dreadful
bastard
Mr. Reality ever comes knocking, make sure to answer the door with a shotgun, throwing knives, pepper spray, foaming both at the mouth and crotch, wearing an eye-patch, stinking of alcohol and dreams, holding all the pretty letters people have sent you…Yeah.

ℛ REFLECTION

You always have to prove yourself
to yourself no
matter what, never enough, when you were younger,
small, thin, light hands you fought the bigger guys, maybe 4 of
them, it doesn't matter, succeeded with a black eye to match the
chipped tooth to match the crooked grin and it continues,
now,
you jump across gaps, off cliffs, over fences, you still manage to
find the biggest,
the worst, the scariest
thing
there is to you and then meet it,

calm,
scared different than normal because inevitability is just that,
you step forward, and there it is,
that ridiculous
full-length mirror
in your bedroom.

෪ EXORCISM

ghosts leave me alone, you bring too much with you, too much I
don't want, leave me alone,

ghosts,

don't smile at me from passing cabs, don't wave at me in
dreams, don't call my name out on subways, make me dash into
the next car, jump off at the next stop, run for the exit, leave me
alone,

ghosts,

don't get my phone number from someone in a bar, don't call
me, don't leave messages,
I will never answer the phone when I see your number on Caller
ID because I'm good with numbers and when I see your number
I add it up and it's bad, it's too much,
I delete your messages without listening, leave me alone,

ghosts,

don't send me emails because I will mark them as junk
without ever opening them, leave me alone, you know I'm
scared of you, leave me alone,

ghosts,

don't trail your scent behind you like you're walking in front of
me on the street,

don't travel ahead of me, leaving a strand of your hair in the sink
of some hotel room

moments

before I check in, leave me alone,

ghosts, I've

already written you fully out of my conscious, partly out of my
subconscious, my waking thoughts have nothing to do with you
and I'd

like to keep it that way, ghosts,

I decline your invitation to a reunion of the living dead,

do not yell at me when I walk past graveyards, leave me alone,
let me be, that

old smile of mine is filled with rotted teeth,

those old jokes of ours

just aren't funny any longer, all that Old Time we spent together
has been replaced

by Present Time and I absolutely refuse to move backwards after
all these years, ghosts, leave me alone... I'm

just

no good

with the past.

ೞ FRIDAY NIGHT WITH ALL THAT SPEED

The Blonde

just puked up most of a gallon of 14-dollar white wine, raviolis
with too much ricotta, half a muscle relaxer- she's moaning in
the bedroom, asking, why, why, why... I filled her water bottle,
put her Newports by the bed, tried undressing her- peeping tom-
it didn't work (she's sleeping in her clothes- poor...) I

turned out the light,

closed the door... crushed the last bit of Aderol and blew a neon orange line right into my already tweaked

fried out

jelly brains... it's Friday night. The Giant passed out around the 18th beer, the Jewish housewife (that's my other friend, hell of a guy) went home stumbling out the door, looking for car keys, beat down, to think of the woman that's ruining him (forget drinking,

she's

what's making him stumble), thinking of himself getting ruined, kicked out of his wedded house to back under the parent's roof, guy's closing in on 30 years breathing, 8 months married and choking, so easily, (the reckless release of drowning) not a fight...ah, the

humanist in me comes out, wants to help him, (friend to beast and man alike – huh, Fante?) he's screwed, shackled, tied, taken down so quickly when he had his head turned to smile at the hired photographer like big game...it was

so sporting of her,

the first steady fuck he's ever had so he's all green around the balls the gills all

about the (autonomous muscle in the wrong place, it's an investment) love, cunt teeth white in all that wasted camera flash in a rented hall with an open bar; tuxedos,

his best friend from high school playing at best man...ah, (not everyone plays fair honey)

(tell me about it)

(even you/me?)?

(with myself? (you) how could I?)

(you know, you're (whispers the subconscious) always fucking yourself over...)

(I know...)

I'm fucked up and trapped just as bad as the next guy. Head, hands, eyes, future, outlook (for a kid like me- fucked) shaky, the keyboard pulls that musical letter bit so that I work on hitting one key, wind up striking another, look at it say, you're no fucking letter N, I meant to type…(john/k---- stop yelling

some people are sleeping, you're)…off the handle. I have to slow myself up,

stop my anger

at the misplaced keys, it's my eyes (breathe deep, try regulating the heart rate (no need to hyperventilate alone in the small room) even though it's been interfered with long before this, and by things way stronger than

your..

(it's natural) self

then around 2 am with everything double vision trails, heart racing having to piss not wanting to get up, picking apart your lines, putting yourself down, pitying, anything with a heart beat (born fucked) one trap or another, something designed for everyone and there's no stopping the falling once you've slipped on that first step ("Imagination

and Roget's intellect

is a banana peel of a virus." says someone laughing in a way that isn't all that comforting (it's your laugh (and it sounds like it

knows

way

too much)

(I know)))…I take a white Bic lighter to my half of the muscle relaxer,

use a bad book as backing, it's *Bailing Water*, (1st

and only edition signed by the author

for what reason- he/me/I couldn't tell you why we do it,) we crush the thing up, remove the plastic coating, pull a bump and stifle a yelp from that harsh pharmaceutical powder burning-boiling tar *bailing water*- 15 year eroded nasal cavity feel in my 28 year old nasal passages...

exhale, lean back with a sigh- what am I doing?

28 at 4 am and drinking in an empty room all alone,

what do you expect

out of New York sweetheart,

an arraignment date on the 25th: misdemeanor marijuana possession in the green tree state of Vermont and that black funk cloud of despair thing has been hovering over me, going on 3 weeks now (the tally of debts; warrants, utility bills, retainers, unfinished stories, poems that explode in your chest and fizzle out across the page ((those always hurt the most) it gets to be

too much after a while) the

pains in your side (under the rib, I know what it means) after a three day (sick call to the office) whisky night) and now sitting on the couch, birds waking up, I try

(real hard honest Indian, not just a boy scout who just wants the pocket knife)

thinking about everything I've ever written (metal,

and curved, that blade...it's inevitable) I try

thinking about the things that actually showed life. The words that amazed me made me double-take myself in the mirror, woke me up in the middle of the night, sent me giggling mad into a 6 am shower crushing beer cans against the ceramic soap dish, john

beyond yourself so naturally, and I look at him/you/me in the mirror, in the reflection of someone's eyes wondering

how to

hold on

to it all....

❧ IT HIDES

once I found it in the trunk

of The Blonde's car while looking for a beach chair;

it was mixed up with a pair of stockings, surrounded by spent tampon

applicators and hair

brush handles…and another time

I found it in a public restroom; I was standing up,

wiping at my ass, examining what I had left behind, and I saw it,

down there with all the muck and the brown and I reached two fingers into the bowl, plucked it out,

dripping toilet water, heavily scented, I

had to wrap it in paper and

put it in my pocket…and once I found it in *The Night Torn Mad with Footsteps*;

but I didn't take it because that would be stealing,

but the next day I did find it in *As I lay Dying* and that seemed alright so I took it and ran (thanks Willy)…then

a few years back

I remember finding it at the bottom of a

gram bag of coke; it was all covered in white, shaking just a little, it

moved

real fast,

like it was trying to get away from something, maybe me, I'm not sure, but I

grabbed it

when no one was looking and

shoved it into my sock…then another time

I caught a glimpse of it while looking in the mirror;

but that one

scared living hell out of me so I left it alone

CЗ IN PREPARATION

with tomorrow bound to happen and the next one
after that as well- with everything waiting, grinning at the
inevitability of you
opening those brown eyes sunshine morning screaming daybreak

it's all out there

and after a toast to the ceiling, (waiting)
I pour out a few sips onto the mattress in

offering

to drunks past and there's
just a (Sunday night)
sip or so
left
'til I smile

CЗ SHE LOOKS AT ME IN THE HAMMOCK

and for the first time since she's ever REALLY (McCuller's)
seen me I look pathetic; down 30 pounds and my eyes have lost
their luster, their kick, my long lashes gone from fireworks
bright yellow-orange Gucci fireworks of thought to hum-drum
automaton somnambulistic (subway tunnel

beat down life) brown (and past that

a conveyor belt of a kid!)

edging

into empty day dreaming (red)…(understanding lower than an
infant's fear of falling- she can tell) that I'm treading water

in a deep ocean, a screwed kid giggling at cliff's edges (Oh muse

you're opening the doors for me and fucking me at the same time
(do you know that?)) and giggling at life rafts, wax wings and
umbrellas in the rain, turning 28 and lost, lost…

(smashed mirror smiling

seven years of…) she looks at me in the hammock, "John honey,
just come down from there. I'll help make it better."

and I wonder

if she knows what she's gotten into.

⌘ OFFERING TO THE GODS

He told her that they were making history. That
forevermore, throughout all of Life and
all of Death, the immortal gods of jizz would
watch over them.

He then forced her arm up,
and behind her back, her face
pressed into the cushion of a car seat, he
yelled something
in Japanese, she squealed
and they both
exploded.

⚕ Who's In Charge?

half-way through the bottle I see it's worked its way down,

now it's just the three of us: Karim; the Arab next door, the work-body, Mr. Provider, the organizational expert that got this thing started (Since I was 4 you fucking asshole- now you credit me?) John;

the

the, well, the eye-candy, the banner man, the poster boy with red eyes with blank grin, with

no cares, and
easy ways and, Me, the Great I, The Typer; the scribe, the kid with worn down fingertips and self-doubt, yet ego, ego, ego (I yell 'Buy my books!' at 4 am

in an empty bar)…but, half-way through the bottle, (dry-heaving into a garbage can)

I switch to beer,
pack the bowl, step outside to smoke Drum tobacco and

forget

about all this shit…

⚕ Argument

So funny- get disgusted by what you see then work it so you see double, get twice as disgusted, "That look on your face when you're watching television, like

you're gonna puke or something." She

calls me pretentious, but I tell her "It's just standards, standards

standards

honey."

❧ Every Waking Second

every waking second it's always there shit breathe eat every particle before I fall asleep I pray ask for just one thing oh please oh help me to keep going keep trying too much dangerous terrible ridiculous it's opening eyes tongue lash your own self for not doing not fulfilling not being THE THING that's been occupying every thought each ejaculation all that squiggling white is your fingers finding a way over walls the only way out for

you

anything else is inconsiderable is completely

fucking

preposterous(!)

is you (reader) reading bilingual newspaper scratching chin saying there's john

'I'd recognize that smell upwind.'

it's desperation by dempsey (vomit anguish self destruction with giggling lots of giggling) the only thing the living breathing globe thing that puts right foot left foot puts august 24 like clock hours no matter the passage no matter the letdown the drop from cliffs each year prompting internal tear apart the itch to flee from body the can't do it pretender playing at just playing you're…

and even with all that the fingers

the fingers still

my fingers still

misbehave explode act on their own convictions…

johnny?

yeah? what you reading there? Yeats. the second coming? that's the one, that line

about 'passionate intensity'

○R CONSTRUCTION PROBLEMS

thoughts
too big for paper "There's just no
infrastructure!"
either that or
I still haven't
figured out
the medium

○R GOALS

I want to write things that make people in Europe jump from
windows,

I want to infect with my words like some typing virus,

I want my poems to force

middle-aged men to hang themselves from

old

warehouses' rafters, I want to write horror, disease, lust, insanity,

I want to write the kind of things that'll turn a catholic school
girl into a meth freak,

have her stay awake for 3 days in a hotel room in Brooklyn

servicing

husbands gone astray, I want to write the kind of things that
people will remember with a look of fear, 'That bastard

typed everyday devils into existence!' I want to write the words
that shake you out of bed with stomach cramps, send you to the
bathroom to crap, then maybe you wipe at your ass with a page

torn out of some anthology

and it's got my name on it, I want to write things that make sexy little

goth girls crawl across all the metal studded, latex encased states to camp out

on my doorstep, (each day I'd pick a new one out to sit on my lap and

she'd

cradle my face, calling me a strangely beautiful and

tragic creature

while I stroke at her pale thighs) I want my keystrokes to be the pulled triggers of firing squads, to be trap doors under praying convicts, I want it all to be like that time I tried painting in high school,

and someone told me that it all starts from inside, just take out a little part of what's in you and put it on the canvas. I want all my paintings

all my words

all my thoughts

to be like that, just a shaky

black line

running

across the page.

⚭ HE SAID

screw the old he said give me

a mountain of percocet and I'll blow sun out the sky I'll make

the new I'll force typewriters in the 1950's jump to past-life just long enough to type my name, I'll make literary legs spread in such a way that in the morning language wakes up, looks around, notices bite marks, starts remembering, becomes frightened, enticed, somehow morning-wet sticky smell of the time she had her first... he said give me the mountain of escape, give me the consistent, the non-stop, the never ending supply of john smiles understanding, the enough to make you (me, I, all of us, yes!) think things are maybe beyond cigarette burns on sweatshirts nodding off on all that percocet he said, give me 12 am itchy scratching till it bleeds I'll sponge it up wring it out make it to be oh so nice and comprehensible, please, so desperate in bed sweating with runny nose worth 7 dollars a drop, he said give me, just...

▧ HOW I LOST MY COPY

I got the phone call in my hotel room,

(The hotel was just outside of Wilmington, VT. I was alone, on a 2-week vacation, traveling through the Green Mountain State. I had my laptop, some clothes, my snowboard, a season pass that was good at 5 different mountains, a bag filled with painkillers, a dozen tall boys, and a half-ounce of pot- ideal.

Matchbook had just come out and I was celebrating; lying naked on the queen-sized bed, drinking tall boys, and

every few minutes

I would pick up the copy that Iriswhite had sent. I'd

look at the name on the cover, see that it belonged to one of my I's,

and start giggling and squeezing at myself.

Then the phone call.)

"Hello?"

"John, I gotta tell you something."

"What happened?"

"Are you sitting down?"

"What happened?"

"Thompson just went the way of Ernie."

Stunned.

Almost a minute before I started breathing again. I asked,

"Are you sure?"

"I wouldn't have called unless I was."

And I hung the thing up. (People always wonder why I'm afraid of ringing telephones. There's

never anything but blackness

being transmitted through that ever-fucking device- just a few words, that's all it takes, and personal worlds become sandcastles at high tide.) All of a sudden,

giggling was out of the question. Instead I just lay there,

thinking about what we had all lost. (Upstairs,

I saw a trail of footsteps ending abruptly,

and

a thousand young typists scratching their heads, all of them asking,

What happened?

Where'd the path go?

How do we follow?)

I

picked up *Matchbook*,

found a pen, and scribbled a quick dedication:

For Hunter-

   I

   can almost understand.

Then I signed it,

threw it under the bed,

and started packing. (And I know I've told you this plenty of times before, but I don't care: I'm afraid of ghosts. Deathly afraid! Seriously. Just thinking about them gives me the shits and I had a feeling that I had just called one up.)

I dialed the number for the front desk and got the hotel manager.

"Yes Mr. Dempsey?"

"I need to switch rooms. Any smoking room will do."

"Is there something wrong with the room sir?"

"It's haunted."

"Is this a joke?"

"No. Bring up an EMF meter and you'll see. Also, there's a shit stain on the mattress. What kind of a place are you guys running here?"

"Are you sure?"

"Positive. Come up and I'll show you. It looks like there's chewing gum in it."

"That won't be necessary Mr. Dempsey. Just come down to the lobby and we'll set you up in a different room."

"But no ghosts or shit stains this time. It's a health violation you know."

"Of course sir."

"Okay, I'll wipe up and come down. Give me 10 minutes."

A little later I got into that different room. Stripped back down to nothing,

and got into bed with the rest of the beer. The

party was over,

and so I just lay there

wondering how it'd go with me

when the time came,

and who would get the phone call when I went, also

if anyone would ever find that

signed copy

under the bed.

⌘ GREAT EXPECTATIONS

Call someone something for

long enough and

they're bound

to live up to it no matter

how much will, backbone, internal drive to go against the grain
they may have

it

happens…

Just try and guess

what I've been called

throughout the years

⌘ HORTICULTURE- PROPAGATION

Everything curling up and rotten inside spreads out same as bad
plant with root rot

I'm the root of my world and as fucked depraved saddened and
impoverished your world may be I say screw your world and all
other worlds and their world's colliding with each other I'm

root rot screw your friend's and girlfriend's worlds screw your
mother's brother's father's sister's worlds…

Barely out of my twenties and already way

too

desperate for my world and dead drunk slugging scotch (water to the plant) on Monday in the mid

afternoon

❦ #3

#3 was something special, she was something dynamic, she was beyond

ME

in so many ways, she was feeling,

imagination,

and abandon all at once, she was

more

than all the ones that had come before her,

almost more than all the ones that came after, she was something untamed, something unclassifiable, she was adventure and heat mixed together;

we drove to Tobay Beach in November, and huddled close

under the docks, watching the surf being kicked up by the waves, pointing out shapes in the foam, discussing things like natural flow while

drinking gin

from a thermos.

huddled close like that, I

pretended to be a businessman,

cheating on his glamorous but cold wife with the artist girl from town.

she played the punk rocker with pierced nipples and a shaved head

full of philosophy,

enlightening the young drunk she had met at a concert.
(imagination, abandon, adventure and heat

mixed together...)

and on the ride home we took turns driving, stretching time from 45 minutes to 3 hours of swerving, unbuttoning, heavy breathing, pulling over onto the shoulder to explode towards each other then

trading places and

starting

all over

again.

she

called me a dichotomy, long before I had ever known what it was, and

a poet, long before I had ever shown her a word, and

eventually,

she called me an asshole for dry humping her friend against the refrigerator in her parent's kitchen but still

Shelly,

I once wrote that you worked like good poetry,

but I never realized

how much truth

was in that statement 'til just now.

ॐ I COULD'VE BEEN

a groundbreaking pornographer

taking pictures of

naked women with a penchant

for

doorknobs, chair legs and bicycle

handlebars with specifically molded grips- nubs

in just

the right places

ॐ #4

#4 was strange business, what she was into

was always from behind- bent over kitchen tables, leaning

against the back of chairs, or in bed, with her face pressed into a
pillow and her asshole undulating, pulsating with anticipation-
strange business- just a little saliva, "Just

spit on it." she said while

smiling over her shoulder (that smile was all hunger,

that smile was all want,

that smile was a

deep, back brain yearning for something other than what she was
born with (I should've known)), and

strange business

became stranger with her new haircut, "Do you like it this
short?", and stranger still,

"Tonight I'm gonna wear a baseball cap." and I didn't see the pattern at first, I was

too

wrapped up

in trying new things (sure, John the open minded with flecks of brown around the head!), then stranger still, "Look what I picked up at the thrift shop. Vest,

tie and everything!"

"And I even have a white button-down shirt!"

"And with a hat, you know, the ones with the brim,

I bet I'd look almost like that guy from

Casablanca! Well,

from behind

anyway." then that smile once again (it

was such an animal thing that I just couldn't resist it), understanding out the window I

did it anyhow…

and then afterwards, laying next to her, the fedora pushed back on her head, she was

smiling at the ceiling, a little bit of that want

satisfied,

and I knew

that I'd never be able to watch

another Bogart movie again.

✿ How We All Became Killers

Commuters stick to schedules. Barring unforeseen events, they take the same train every morning, and come home on the same train every night. The day after all this happened I caught a later train than usual. And while waiting on that later train I saw a lot of the people from the day before; the guy with the cell phone, the girl I almost bit, the woman with the pocketbook, and every one of them had the same expression on their face.

It was the same expression that I saw when I looked in the mirror that morning. It reminded me of when I was 12, and my mother snuck up behind me while I was pissing in a neighbor's mailbox. There was no way I could deny what I had done.

***

I caught the 3:27. Destination: Syosset. ETA: 4:22. That gave me more than enough time to get home, make the bank before they closed- withdraw, withdraw, withdraw- and meet the pill kid at 5:30. By 6 I'd be in The Land of Nod. Wednesday night. Fantastic.

I found an open seat next to the emergency exit window- survivalist that I am, just in case something happened, I didn't like the thought of depending on some flabby bitch or businessman to open the thing up. Then I popped 500 milligrams between my teeth, chewed, swallowed, opened up *Port of Saints*, and waited.

I was waiting for those 500 milligrams to kick in. I was waiting for my thoughts to slow down, for my spine to go limp; it was all on its way. Just a few more minutes and I would slump into the seat, my eyelids would get heavy, my neck would bend, my chin would fall into my chest, but then, out of nowhere, I started to have a bad feeling.

(I smelled something coming off the tracks ahead of the train and it was the same smell that I caught that night on Pulaski Rd., when I was with The Blonde and we saw the kid standing in the middle of the street, pointing towards a tree, and under the tree was another kid, pale, motionless, a little blood leaking out from between his open lips.) It made me uneasy.

I looked around the train. It was packed with the working class (I've never considered myself a part of that group, "Me? Way too enlightened for all that mess." said John the pretentious.); the suits, the skirts, the leather bagged, shiny shoed, clock punching, cock sucking mass of warped humanity.

Their faces showed The New York Times, The Wall Street Journal, 2-storey houses, children in expensive day care centers, Caribbean vacations, nice restaurants, plastic surgery, prostate exams, but for all their adjustment and well being, that dark smell from up ahead, just hadn't reached their nostrils yet.

I wasn't worried though; I knew I was the only canary onboard. I was ahead of the curve. Sure. Everybody else had jizz in their brains. Not me though.

As the train pulled into Jamaica Station the smell got heavier. I picked up a hint of something like Time that hasn't yet been unraveled and so I knew it was a future smell. There was also a touch of Fate mixed into the scent and that let me know there was no avoiding whatever it was; Something Dark Up Ahead- that's a good name for a cologne for black guys.

There's a 4 minute window between the train's arrival and departure from Jamaica Station. I rolled a cigarette, left my book bag on the seat to show that it was taken, and stood smoking on the platform. I tried to think of what could possibly smell so dark, what kind of animal, in what kind of situation, would release that kind of scent? I had no idea, but I suddenly realized that I felt a little bit like Hemingway.

I pitched the cigarette butt under the train and boarded just as the doors were closing. Then I made my way up the aisle to my seat. When I got there I saw something that I didn't like.

It was about 250 pounds of bald businessman, sitting in my seat and talking on his cell phone. My book bag was on the floor, shoved under the seat and his feet were resting on it. He was in the middle of a conversation. From the way he shook when he spoke it looked heated.

"But I told those fucking painters blue for the bathrooms! Shit! What's their number?"

"Hey. Guy." That's me.

"4387- Right."

"Hey. Jackass."

He was oblivious. There was no one else in the world but himself and the person on the other end of the line.

"I'm not paying for that paint job. You gave them a check, right?"

"Hey, you big tub of shit."

He didn't even flinch and so I reached out and jabbed a finger into his shoulder. It sank in 2 inches, just like if I had poked it into a pillowcase filled with yogurt or old sour cream or something.

Suddenly the guy's world of two opened up to allow someone else into it. Me. He turned in the seat and for the first time I got a look at his face. It was a pale purple color. I saw his open mouth, the vibration of chins and acne scars on his cheeks. His eyes were a worn out grey streaked through with red.

There was hair hanging out of his nose. There were veins bulging out of his temples. He had no earlobes. There was a brown mole on his neck. I saw the whole mess of the person that he was. I saw it magnified and multiplied and it was the same as staring into the frothing mass of any major city from a high vantage point.

"What do you want?"

"You're in my seat."

"It was empty when I got on the train."

"It's my seat. That's my bag that you shoved under it. Get up tubby."

"What was that?"

"Get the fuck up and get the fuck out of that seat before there's a problem."

"It wasn't me that shoved your bag under there."

"I don't care. Get up."

"You don't have to be rude."

It figures. Someone pulls a move like that, and then has the cum-faced nerve to call you rude.

"Get the fuck up guy."

Then we just looked at each other. He was probably thinking about what he was capable of. He outweighed me by no less than 70 pounds, but crazy beats size almost every time -Dempsey! He figured it out, got up, and shuffled his bulky ass down the aisle. As he was walking away I heard him talking into his cell phone.

"I was just assaulted by some lunatic. I think he was a Spic."

I sat down, avoided the stares of the other people, and opened up *Port of Saints* for the second time. The encounter had taken my mind off that dark smell coming from up ahead, but as soon as I settled into the seat I got hit by another whiff. Then a whistle blew, wheels turned, the train picked up speed, and those 500 milligrams finally kicked in.

I started to relax as all that pharmaceutical magic worked its way through my body. I stopped trying to read, and just stared out the window.

The scenery zipped past the window as the train sped through the scenery. I realized that it was a symbiotic relationship and congratulated myself on my powers of perception. Then I smelled it again. This time it was strong.

I looked around the train, but it still didn't seem as if anybody else noticed it. Then a small part of me spoke up with a small voice that said one word, Fear, and I suddenly became scared. That's how these things work. That small part knew there was something to be sacred of up ahead, something tragic and damaging to self, something that I shouldn't take any part in, but was speeding towards with the inevitability of all things unavoidable.

Through the window I saw the track curve out and to my left. Past the curve was an intersection point where the track met the street. I followed the track with my eyes, saw the flashing gates, heard the clanging bells, and as we got closer, I saw one of the gates bouncing up and down, like something was blocking it.

Suddenly my view was cut off and the train let out a long, loud whistle. I was jolted forward in my seat as the engineer hit the brakes. My nose filled up with that dark smell, and then the crunching-in-on-itself sound of one stationary metallic object meeting a much bigger unstoppable metallic object tore through the train.

After that there was silence. Everybody looked around the car trying to figure out what had happened. One woman held a hand to her nose. There was blood dripping off her fingers. Somewhere towards the front of the car a child was crying. I saw the guy who had tried taking my seat earlier standing in the aisle, talking on his cell phone.

"I think it may have been terrorists."

And then I simply nodded off.

(Strong pills don't really care about things like dark smells or train crashes; they're unsympathetic and goal oriented, kind of like some of the people you can find in any financial district around the world, the ones with substandard insides.)

When I heard the first siren I came out of my stupor. Then the conductor came on over the loudspeaker.

"We apologize for the delay folks. There has been a collision with a car that was stuck on the tracks and we are waiting for police and medical assistance."

People were at the windows, trying to see what was going on outside of the train, trying to catch a glimpse of what was giving off that dark smell.

I stayed in my seat, with my nose tucked into the collar of my shirt.

After a few minutes the sirens stopped and that sound was replaced by the flashing of lights. Assistance had arrived. The train began to back up. The conductor came on over the loudspeaker once again.

"We are returning to New Hyde Park until the tracks can be cleared. Once again, we apologize for this inconvenience."

I snickered and the woman with the bloody nose gave me a dirty look- she didn't get the joke.

The train backed up about 100 feet and stopped. The doors opened, and everybody surged out onto the platform. Some people ran for the line of waiting taxis, others looked around, dazed, unsure of their next move, while others called people on their cell phones.

I didn't want to waste money on a cab, I was doped out, but not dazed, and I don't own a cell phone. Instead I leaned against the hand railing that ran the length of the platform, rolled a cigarette, and lit it. I was definitely doped out.

An hour later an announcement was made, saying that the tracks couldn't be cleared and that buses had been rerouted in order to pick us up.

Another hour after that people started shoving each other, bumping each other, cursing and fighting to cram into the buses. When I got shoved I shoved back. When I got bumped I bumped back. I elbowed a skinny kid in glasses when he tried to step around me, and almost bit the back of a young girl's leg as she was stepping onto the bus. Eventually, I got on too.

Standing room only! Right up front by the driver! Fantastic! The doors closed behind me, trapping a pocketbook. The owner of the pocketbook started beating at the doors and tugging until the thing got loose. Then the bus moved for half a block before coming to a stop. Looking through the windshield I saw why.

There was a traffic jam, lots of flashing lights, and that dark smell got so heavy I almost gagged. Little by little the bus crept forward, gaining on the smell... (And to think that I had a front row seat, so fantastic, seriously, it was really

so

fucking fantastic.)

A policeman waved the bus through the intersection. About 5 miles an hour. And I got a good, long look at the scene.

The scene: It was a crushed blue something with lots of red on the side of it. There was a fireman on top of the blue thing and he was working with what looked like a circular saw, trying to cut the blue thing in half. As he moved the saw a spray of red came up and hit him in the face, and then began leaking out all around the blue thing. There was lots of it; a puddle of it and it was growing, spreading wider, and I had the feeling that if that puddle spread fast enough, and if the bus tires rolled through it, I would have to scream.

I suddenly had the thought that if I hadn't been on the train, then all that red wouldn't be here. That it was my fault somehow. That I had contributed to it and that my contribution was essential for making all this happen. I looked away from the scene, and scanned the faces of the other people on the bus. Their expressions said that they had just had the same exact thought.

As soon as we passed through the intersection the bus driver made an announcement.

"Once again we apologize for this inconvenience."

But this time- as funny as it was, that word they kept using, 'inconvenience', like that's all it was- I didn't snicker.

◌ѯ I COULD'VE BEEN

an ivy league

son of a bitch, graduated

at the top of my class with a degree in finance, millions

in the bank, the big house, a stock portfolio, my name listed in Forbes and a plastic

wife to

cheat on

ᛒ WHY TRAINS?

Why do so many of your stories, poems, rants involve trains?

Because that's what I know. I'm always on trains. I spend hours riding in one direction, and then hours riding in the opposite direction- every day! I can call up the image of these trains without thought. I can be miles away- in Panama, Amsterdam, New Orleans- and smell the disinfectant used to clean the bathrooms. I can hear commuters talking, snoring, farting, scratching at their snatches while I'm in a movie theater. I can sit on my couch and read off the advertisements on all the billboards from Syosset to Penn Station. I write what I know about.

But still. How about some variety? Why not write about cowboys? Or pedophiles? People like stuff like that.

I do.

Not enough though. It's always trains. Trains killing people. Trains being delayed and screwing you up from making the bank. Trains where someone is jerking off into a coffee cup. It's too much.

What are you talking about, too much? Don't tell me what's too much. I'm the writer. I'm the one with the fingers and the keystrokes. I call the shots. Who the hell are you?

Me? I'm the main critic. I'm the highest authority. I'm the small voice in your center, and believe me, Mr. Writer, Mr. Keystroke, you shouldn't talk to me like that.

Why not?

Because I'll make you hate yourself.

Too late! The globe beat you to that. Years ago! You're Johnny come late while the audience snoozes with their legs spread. You're a jack-off artist without an old sock to his name. Do you think you can scare me?

Then I'll make it worse. Worse than you thought possible. All these years, I've just been toying with you, just giving you a taste. Remember that.

You couldn't possibly make it any worse. Besides, I don't believe in critics- main or not, internal or outside of myself. They're for people who actually care about the opinions of others. I'm not one of those guys.

You really think so?

I know so! I'm self-centered. I'm the focal point of the universe. Hell, even the sun takes second place when I step into the picture.

Ah, you've got a lot to learn Johnny boy. What do you think happens when you close your eyes? Who do you think's in charge then? Huh? Me. I'm the one whispering in your ear at night. I'm the one responsible for all that self-loathing, and I'm the one responsible for all your self-worship. I'm your string puller. You've read Pavlov. What do you think's gonna happen if you don't listen to me?

(And of course I don't listen. This guy's nuts if he thinks he can scare me into cowboys and pedophiles. I don't know anything about cowboys, or pedophiles. I know about trains. And drinking, drugs, sex. I know about myself. String puller or not, main critic or not, midnight whisper all he wants, this guy's got another thing coming, I'm

John the

un-

intimidate-able! Just watch. Cue up a train story. I even know which one- Roger. And let's see what happens.)

ROGER

Roger hesitated for a moment, and then the train swung around a turn in the tracks and right before her body pressed into his, he managed to get his arm around her. At first his arm hovered, less than an inch away from her shoulder, and then it seemed like she snuggled into him and that gave him courage. He slowly lowered his arm until it rested on her shoulder, his hand almost cupping the bicep.

(I'm the one who set it all into motion, and then I watched it all happen. I'm God. I'm a peeping tom. I'm the all powerful hand on the controls. I'm the director, and I'm also the editor and audience. All the actors are puppets; living, breathing puppets with strings tied to their arms, legs, thoughts and hearts. If you haven't figured it out yet, I'm the master string puller.

Welcome to Dempsey's Playhouse!

A theater with one seat- reserved for me- and a stage that stretches out towards the infinite! Fantastic!)

Roger looked down at the sleeping girl and wondered what her name was. He thought it might be Dawn, or Sherry, something that would match her pale skin and small mouth. Then the train jerked, and he froze, holding his breath, scared that she might wake up. He counted to thirty, and when she didn't wake up, Roger started breathing again.

He had seen the girl a hundred times while sitting on this train in the morning. He looked for her every day, and always tried to sit as close to her as possible. The closest he had ever gotten was last week, when he found himself sitting across from her, with only four feet of empty space between them. Roger remembered how nervous he had been. How the sweat started at his armpits and ass when she looked over at him and smiled.

(When it came to casting I looked for a somewhat heavyset guy to play Roger. I chose someone that weighed a little over 200 pounds, and stood less than six feet tall. His face was pasty, but clear, and his eyes are blue, his hair is thin, and I can tell you he's never had a girlfriend.

I gave him a past. I had him graduate college a year early even though he wasn't very smart. I made him industrious. I had him spend all his nights and weekends studying while everybody else drank beer, smoked pot, and stuck fingers inside their classmates. I got him a job as soon as he graduated, as an accountant at a finance company.

Then I made it so he lived with his mother until he was 29, paying off the mortgage on her house from his paychecks. Then, once the mortgage had been paid off, I had him move into a small apartment that was neat, and nicely (but not expensively) furnished, and there were lots of windows that let in sunlight.)

Roger concentrated on not sweating. He replayed the conversation he had dreamed of having with the girl. It was more than just a conversation; it was the story of how he had finally found someone. And not just any someone, but the right someone. The someone he had been looking for ever since he had gotten his first pubes, ever since the first night he had spit into his palm, ever since those first drops of liquid pearl had shot out from between his fingers and into his consciousness.

Here's how it played out in his mind: One morning he would stand behind the girl while they were waiting for the train. When the train pulled up he would grab her arm, gently, but with determination. She would turn around and look at him, not saying anything. He would hold her while all the other commuters moved around them. Then, once the train pulled out of the station, and they were standing alone on the platform, he would say,

"I'm sorry I did that, but I have to talk to you."

And then he would launch into it without giving her a chance to say anything until he had finished.

"All I know is that you have dark hair, pale skin, blue eyes and that your nose is small and covered with freckles and that they're small too. Your mouth is small, your ears are small and you have two holes in the right one. I know you wear a white coat, and dress pants and that you have three different pairs of work shoes. I know there is something inside of you that is kind of like a magnet, and it's also kind of like the sun and then sometimes it's also like a bird. I know when I see you I get nervous and then I spend the rest of the day thinking about you, thinking of how I should've talked to you. I know that right now, more than anything else in the world, all I want is to kiss you. And even though I've never kissed a woman before, I know that it would work out. That I'd all of a sudden know how to kiss the second I knew that you wanted to be kissed by me. And then I'd like to take you home and make you breakfast so that we could talk to each other. What do you think?"

In Roger's dream she would smile up into his face, her eyes would close, and they would kiss long and slow and there wouldn't be any drool or awkwardness when his tongue met hers somewhere in the dark.

(I also made sure that Roger was something of a poet. He didn't actually write any poetry, he just thought in poetry. But when he opened his mouth to talk to people, especially girls, like the one sitting next to him on the train, I made it so that all he could say was uh, um, excuse me, and then I made it so that his face got red and forced him to walk away with his heart pounding like madness in his chest- I'm a dick like that.

I figure if the guy pulling my strings believes in continuously fucking over his puppets, then why the hell can't I?)

Roger thought about his dream, and knew it would never happen. Even with all those great lines rumbling around in his head, as soon as he started to speak his tongue would call mutiny, curl up onto itself, and lay like some hibernating frog in his mouth. He felt inadequate and foolish. He knew pretty girls like this didn't pay any attention to him- no way- nice guys that knew how to treat women the right way, make them feel special, wanted, needed; there's simply no demand for something like that, not in this century.

He knew all they wanted were guys who dressed nicely, that had good faces and bodies that came from rich parents and drank and ran around with women. They wanted bad boys that could turn into husbands so they could divorce them down the line and ask for alimony.

He knew this because he was the exact opposite of all those things and never once had any girl or woman ever shown any interest in him. Every time he saw one of them on the street or in a store, he would send out the following message with his mind: Are you looking for a good person? Do you want someone that you could talk to and who would listen instead of just tuning you out? Do you want someone who will respect you? Do you want someone you could grow with and laugh with and share thoughts with? Do you want someone that will provide for you and care for you? Do you want someone like me?

And he was always met with stares that quickly appraised him- saw his thinning hair, his pudgy face, his big stomach, and his bland clothes- and then pass over him as if he was a doorknob or a handrail or something- just a fixture.

The train was closing in on Penn Station.

Roger didn't want that to happen. For the first time since he was a small kid he was actually happy, not just content, but no shit, sunshine on your face and money in your pocket happy. He felt the warmth of the girl, and the movement of her body that came with her breathing. He wanted to spend the next hour, more than that, the rest of the day, week, year, his whole life, just like this, just holding this pretty girl while she slept.

(And even though that's possible, even though I could just will it, just think it, just move my fingers and make it happen, I won't. I could make the train a special train that could bend and hold Time and do whatever it wanted just so Roger could be happy for a while, but I won't do that either.

I told you I was a dick. I also told you I was God, but now I take back both. I'm only a little bit of a dick, so that makes me a demigod. I've got this ridiculous thing inside of me that knows the difference between right and wrong on a human level. I could never be the big man upstairs, never THE string puller.)

The train made its way into the tunnel that runs beneath the Hudson River and the car that Roger sat in went dark. In the darkness he leaned over and breathed deep the smell of the girl's shampoo. He then thought to move his arm, but was scared of waking her up. Out of nowhere an idea bloomed in his head, and he found that for once in his life he felt something like courage in his chest. Instead of moving his arm he would pretend to be asleep. That way he wouldn't have to worry about waking the girl, or letting her go too soon.

Roger closed his eyes and forced his breathing into a rhythmic pattern.

(Remember, I'm only a little bit of a dick, just a demigod...)

The girl first felt the man who was hugging her go tense, and then his breathing changed. She knew that they were in the tunnel because of the pressure on her ears. Any moment now the train would stop, and then she would have to get up.

She wasn't sure what would happen after that, she didn't want to think that far ahead. Instead she kept her eyes closed; still pretending to be asleep, and snuggled in closer to the man she had been dreaming about ever since she first saw him 6 months ago. It was something about his eyes, that and the roundness of his face; it was like a full moon and somehow that made it seem as if he was good person.

☙ SELF-APPRAISAL (IN ANSWER TO GOOD OLD MR. HENRY, THE ITALIAN POET)

all the words you've ever written
all the things you've ever felt

all the girls you've ever kissed, made promises to, then screwed on fishing docks, park benches, inside deserted

telephone booths

all the tests you've ever failed, cheated on, then passed with negative results

all the 4 am car rides to the Bronx

all the drugs you've ever dreamt of while tossing in bed with a
hard on

all those midnight
drunken

conversations on street corners with old loves, and long

dead friends

all the awkward mornings in the mirror eyes screaming
'Monster! Idiot! Asshole! Good for nothing

john that you are!' all the guts you've ever spilt, all the blank
screens you've ever

been faced with the same screens that have been following you
from day one, from inception

all these things that WILL NEVER, CAN NEVER

EVER,

be changed they're

what make you

the great escape artist

that you are today.

CR SELF ASSURANCE

everything's all jumbled up in its own philosophy,

confused from its own purpose, freaked out when it looks in the
mirror, no way I'm alone, everything's crazy, itchy (snake
shedding skin I'm snake world's skin), every thing/body, all of
it's got to be just as inside-out confused with it all enough to stop
your heart for a second (many seconds multiple lifelong domino
effect of seconds) all scared, curious, dumbfuckingfounded by
breathing the same airspace as every one else that isn't you and
all that knowing it isn't you and worst of all

all that dreaming tailed by all that knowing that most
everything's also working- maybe even
double hard,

triple hard overtime shift working- to make sure, positive
hundred percent proof sure that dreams (your dreams specifically
yes your dreams you) they never will- on any plane there is, ever
has been, ever will be- never even for the tinniest bit of any Time
be any thing

beyond dreams, you're…you're
just like everyone else, (yes) sure, I'm (the both of us, me, you,
we're both)

so

sure of it

ᏟᎡ YOUR OWN

The madness

lying

inside of an alarm clock. You

don't even have to open your eyes, just

inhale

and you can smell it. Early

in the morning (the dream

gone to nightmare, the nightmare

transformed

into physical

surroundings) it's

all about murder. Maybe even…

CR UNDERSTANDING

There were 2 bottles on the shelf- one dealt in milligrams, the other in fluid ounces- and I was in bed, with lights off, and maybe they thought I was asleep.

"If you take care of the day, then I'll kill the night." said fluid ounces to milligrams.

"Well, if you can take care of Life,

I'll work on killing Time." said milligrams to fluid ounces.

"And if you take care of feeling, I'll work on killing thought."

"Okay, and if you can..."

But I didn't let them finish. I flew out of bed, pointed a finger.

"You treasonous bastards!"

The bottles jumped back, looked as scared and as guilty as any bottle I've ever seen. They started shaking. One went glug-glug. The other rattle-rattle. And I had just finished reading Robert Graves, *Claudius the God*.

"How dare you! Murderers! Usurpers!"

"But we were just..."

"It was..."

"Shut up!"

I wrapped the bed sheet around myself, toga style, and started pacing back and forth in front of the shelf. I rubbed my chin, weighing leniency against tyranny, thinking of my people; the great citizens of I.

"I heard the whole thing. You were plotting against the throne! The both of you. Against your own country!"

"No, we were only..."

"Nothing!"

(Just then there was a knock against the door, and I clearly heard The Blonde, "What the hell are you doing in there?"

"Nothing kitty cat, I'll be out in a minute."

"Why is the door locked?"

"I'm taking care of something."

"But who are you talking to?"

"My subjects!"

"What?"

"Nothing!"

"You're jacking off in there! You're gross!")

I turned my attention back to the shelf.

"Now, for the crime of treason, I sentence the both of you..."

"No!"

"Please!"

("John, let me in already!"

"Quiet, you insolent little... I'm fucking ruling in here!"

"What did you just call me?")

The bed sheet had slipped off my shoulder. I adjusted it before reading their sentence.

"Begging will not save you!"

"But emperor!"

"Banishment!"

"No!"

"Yes! Banishment to the void!"

("C'mon, open up.")

I opened my mouth,

("Are you doing something weird in there?")

gave them a few seconds to collect their last thoughts,

("John, I'm gonna leave if you don't open this door right now!")

then grabbed them both at the same time- iron fisted ruler that I am- and

("You're a real dick, you know that?")

sent them both into the void. Then I opened the door. The Blonde stood there, smoking a Newport, looking both pissed off and beautiful. She was wearing a long white skirt, a red t-shirt with a faded sunflower imprinted on the front, and I had the feeling maybe she wasn't wearing panties.

She hit the light switch, looked at the 2 empty bottles on the shelf, then at the bed sheet that was still wrapped around me. Her head shook back and forth, and then she smiled.

❧ THOSE 4 HORRIBLE WOMEN ON THE TRAIN

I see them every morning. Those 4. They're a pack. Like dogs. But even worse. They're rude and dogs aren't capable of that.

Those 4 horrible women, the whores of 3 decades ago they're worse than rude, they're the types that think they own whatever space they step into, it's all theirs, no one else counts, everybody else is background, just scenery without a pulse.

Those 4 horrible bitches get on the train in the morning, push their way up the aisle, talking loud, talking about their lives, their wasted youth, their mongoloid children, the deals they got while shopping the night before, and they're ugly, their faces sag, their bodies sag, they've been used up and now they try using me up too.

Those 4 horrible women open their mouths and what comes out is death on the ears, shatters my thoughts, is enough to repulse the most perverted person you know, is painful to say the least.

Just listen to them, the one talking now, she's holding a tiny pink paper shopping bag, Victoria's Secret,

"You won't believe the price I paid for this teddy."

and she pulls it out of the bag, it's black, lacy, cut at the right places, even sexy until you picture the hag holding it actually wearing it, and me, the kid who's always tucking it under his belt, the kid that gets hard when he sticks his finger into a cream-filled donut, even I get disgusted.

Then one of the others, one of the 4, she chirps in,

"I could strut around the house wearing that in the middle of the afternoon, I could bend over pretending to pick something off the floor, and James wouldn't even notice me. He'd ask me to fix him a drink, or whether or not I walked the dog that morning."

No kidding. James is either her husband, or the pool boy, or maybe even one of her mongoloid children. This one she's got the figure of, of, well, nothing can be compared to it, she's got the figure of a horrible bitch on a train at 7:30 in the morning.

Thick arms, legs, no neck, the belly, sticking out all around so that she doesn't even walk, just teeters, barely able to control her movements once set into motion

(Ah! I found a comparison, she's built like a bowling ball, but whatever or whomever, would stick their fingers in those holes has got to be one hell of a loony bastard.) ass the size of a car's dashboard and her pants are always stuck in that dashboard ass crack, 2 inches at the least, and she's always digging it out, manicured nails disappearing into the depths.

It makes me choke on my coffee, makes me spit up bile, those nails disappear, they're followed by the first knuckle, then the second, and if she's wearing a ring, well, that vanishes too and she chuckles the whole time, like it's a trick to dig at your ass in the morning while walking up the aisle and she's the only one capable of pulling it off with such flare.

Then another one opens up, another one of the 4 horrible bitches, and she's worse than the ones I've just told you about, this one is vulgar beyond what's acceptable, even by my standards, listen up,

"I know exactly what you're talking about. I have these jeans, and I put them on and I know that my ass looks fantastic. I mean, I've checked it in the mirror, and I'll walk around the mall in that sheer tank top I bought, I mean, you can see the whole works, and I still can't get a man to notice me. I swear, sometimes I think that this whole world's gone gay. That they're all twinks and faeries."

She's crazy. She's an old bitch in heat but even the randiest, un-neutered, cunt craziest animal you could think of wouldn't come sniffing around at her box.

I've seen her in that tank top once before, and her nipples are the business end of piss clams dug up on the beach, I've seen her in those jeans and her ass is 2 balloons filled with yogurt and tied together, her mouth is wide, filled with slanted teeth and her tongue is gray, like she's sucked a lot in her youth and all that jizz stained the pink right off of it, a whitewash, she follows it up with,

"Do you remember how tight we used to be when we were 17? I swear, I look at my daughter and wish I had her snatch. Just for one night."

I gag and almost lose it while those 4 horrible bitches go oh so giddy with laughter, but behind all that laughter is the memory of rubber bands that've given up the ghost of elasticity.

Their laughter covers up their knowledge of being wasted, used, broken beyond repair because not only have they become physically exhausted, but their brains are also shot to shit, all their thoughts are shit particles just clinging to ass hairs, each new thought they have requires a wipe, and this train ride is an enema for them.

This is how they flush themselves out, this is how they get that brown out of their neural pathways, but it's never enough, everyday they're in need of yet another enema, another cleansing, those 4 horrible bitches on the train never stop.

The next one- she squirms around in her seat for about 20 seconds before diving into her crotch and scratching like her panties are laced with leaves of poison ivy,

"It's either the new shaving cream I'm using, or those antibiotics I was on last week. I must've dumped a tube and a half of Monistat into myself last night, but it hasn't had any effect. Maybe I picked something up from that…"

And that's when I realize that I've had my fill, I look at those 4 horrible women, and I'm about to let loose on them, tell them off in such a way, call them such names, really give it to them, so bad, that they'll never again open their mouths on the train or in public, I'm about to do it.

I get my tongue ready, I know the words that'll make them ashamed of themselves, no question about it, I'm good at this stuff, here it comes…

Instead, I stand up and move to the next car. Not a word comes out of me.

Those 4 horrible women, they could be any of my old girlfriends just a few years down the line.

℘ PRACTICE MAKES PERFECT

When I got on the E, uptown, W 4th, I saw a crowd on both ends of the car, but the middle was empty. I've always disliked crowds and so John in the middle it was.

I made my way past the strap-hangers, pole jockeys and semen fiends that can be found on most any subway this side of the city.

"I got 2 bags of crack, and I got a bottle, and I got a pack a cigarettes! So what!"

The reason the middle of the car was empty.

A white guy. He looked younger than 40. He was dressed nicely; you could tell that his clothes cost money, nothing off-the-rack, handmade business, all of it, but in need of a wash. Also jewelry, a gold watch, gold bracelet, rings, a chain. The briefcase next to him, looked like real soft leather.

All in all, he had lost his grip. Slipped. Opened a door, went down a hall, and got lost in the maze. I could tell. There was a fifth of Gordon's, a few sips away from empty, in his hand. He pointed at me first.

"I'm you!"

Then he pointed at an Asian woman.

"And I'm you!"

Then he pointed at a young black kid.

"And I'm you!"

Pointing up and down the train, at every one of the hangers, jockeys and fiends, "I'm you! And I'm you! And I'm you!"

Most everyone got off at 14th, transferred to the A, not me though, I'm a recorder.

At 23rd some more people got on, new faces, fuel to the fire,

"And I'm you! And I'm you! I'm every one of you!"

Then 34th Street, Penn Station, police on the platform, they rush into the car, handcuffs ready. I was looking to catch the 3:27, so I couldn't stick around for the finale. I just heard it happening,

"But I'm you! I'm you! Why would you arrest yourself?"

And then I was home.

I chewed up 2 hits of percocet, snorted another one, and drank enough beer to give me the courage to stand in front of the full-length mirror in my bedroom. I slowly brought up my index finger, opened my mouth, and whispered,

"I'm you."

❧ COMPUTER CRASHES WHEN I'M TYPING

might as well be

car accidents

and tie dyed (Ken Kesey I'm numb

and dying) yellow cliff scenes- 'There should be a

man with

an orbit

that screams

my name

and he's got a stun gun or

tranquilizer darts

something

that stops me

from putting so many things

up my nose.'

❦ ALMOST

I won't say the things needed to get you to stop crying.

I won't retaliate when you slap me.

I won't answer when you curse at me, call me worthless, self-centered and

rotten. The

only thing I can do is

stare at your ass

as you

walk away.

CR #5

It was the smell that woke me up. I was on a couch in the living room in an apartment on the Upper West Side. I looked around.

There were people sleeping on the floor, in chairs, under tables, all over the place. There were overflowing ashtrays, empty beer bottles and dime bags- the aftermath of a party from the night before, and the hostess, #5, she said it was okay if everybody stayed the night- but all that is secondary.

Just setup.

That scent is what matters. And it wasn't my nose that did the work, it was more like my cock had nostrils. I rolled off the couch, heard her grunting in the bedroom, and even with those 6 inches sticking out in front of me (morning wood) I'm still a gentleman, and so I knocked on the door.

"Yeah?"

"You alright in there?"

"Uh. It's this stupid window. I think it's painted shut."

The door was only half closed. I walked in. Saw her. She's fresh out of the shower, wearing a short pink terrycloth bathrobe, and she's struggling with the window, bent at the waist, the bathrobe rising and falling and every time it rose the smell got stronger, 6 inches became 7, and I moved in behind her.

"Here, let me give you a hand with that."

"I don't know why they would paint a window shut like this. It's ridiculous."

But I knew better than that. The way she pressed her ass into me. A stuck window. Sure. They all have their excuses. Their games. They don't want to come right out and ask for it. Scared that maybe they'll be mistaken for easy lays, or nymphomaniacs, or that you'll tell dirty stories about them to your friends, or maybe even that you'll write about them more than a decade later while remembering.

A stuck window, a running toilet, a light bulb that's burnt out-who needs the superintendent when you've got a houseguest with a hard-on and a reputation as a world class crotch eater, finger diddler, nipple tweaker- sure. She knew all about me. Probably from one of her dirty friends.

(I had laid 3 of them that summer, and each one would scream my name while masturbating years later.)

Well, I can play games too- John the handyman without a toolbox! I yank at the window a couple of times, not really trying to open the thing.

"It's definitely stuck. I don't know if I can get it open without a razor blade or screwdriver or something."

"What a shame. It's so nice outside. And this room is so stuffy. Let me try again."

And once again the bathrobe rising, the grunting, the scent, summertime in New York and to hell with red roses, a real horticulturalist pisses in the garden, and spreads fertilizer indoors.

"Wait! I have an idea!"

And she rushes out of the room, brushing against me on the way past, pretending that 7 inches of stiff cock hadn't just made contact with her thigh. She comes back with a folding chair,

"Do you think if I stood on it I'd get more leverage?"

"It's worth a shot."

"Just hold the chair steady."

She says this with all the innocence she can muster. One game after another. She climbs up on the chair, bends over to get a grip on the window, and gentleman or not, play coy all you want, the bottom half of her ass was just under my nose.

I saw curly hairs and noticed that the inside of her thighs were glistening. I reached out a finger, and touched right where it was real shiny- water just isn't that slippery- and then I reached further, upward, inward, and she turned around, still standing on the chair, bent over, but no longer looking so innocent.

ℂℛ #6

(word of mouth)

"I heard what you did that morning after the party."

"What are you talking about?"

"Don't play stupid. She told me all about it. She said that you forced her to do some pretty terrible things."

"Hey, she wanted to do all of those things. If anyone was forced it was me."

"She said that she had bruises on her ass."

"She's crazy."

"I saw her that day. Every time she went to sit down she made a face. She said that you practically raped her."

"No way. You know me better than that. I'm a gentleman."

"Yeah, I know you John. I also know that gentlemen don't leave those kinds of bite marks on nice girls."

"Nice girls? Ha! There's no such thing and you know it."

"Hey! I'm a very nice girl."

"Well, then you're the exception."

"I am. I'm extremely nice. Haven't I always been nice to you?"

"The nicest."

"Didn't I loan you money that time when you had to go to court?"

"Didn't I pay you back?"

"No. But I don't care. And you know why?"

"Why?"

"Because we're friends. Aren't we John?"

"Best friends."

"And friends do favors for each other, don't they?"

"Yeah, I guess so."

"Well I kinda need a favor from you."

"Like what?"

"When I woke up this morning I heard the faucet dripping, and I tried everything but it just won't turn off. Do you think…"

And there it was. I hung up the phone, got dressed and made my way over to her apartment. I knocked, and she answered the door, wrapped in a towel, her hair still wet.

❧ FOLLOWING IN HIS FOOTSTEPS

He smelled it
then I smelled it- I was
just further downwind-

and when I got to it
he was just
rolling off,
his
red rocket

slinking back

❧ THE COMPLIMENT

don't you remember when you were young, maybe 5 years old, and a great man, the

greatest man you have ever known, the one who worked intelligence for a foreign government, the genius, the theoretician, the one who saw more death,

and war,

than you could ever imagine, don't you remember how he once told you

that you were,
by far,
the most destructive
person

he had ever met?

ᙢ GAMBLING

playing cards I've noticed
that some women will bring their sex to the table when playing
with men, they

wear low-cut shirts, thongs that
show when they bend over, they don't
put their chips in the pot, they bet with nipples, lips, dark
curly hairs, and even though

I know that, I

find myself
saying 'All in'
while holding a pair of 3's and a hard-on.

ᙢ WE WERE CLAMS

We were clams, thought the young man while staring at Kim's body, she

let me inside, I mean, she opened up to me, she accepted me, we
made it, were a single thing, cards on the table, nothing else up
our sleeves, shells laid aside, we saw

what we were made of, all the guts for the picking, no more
doors, no more walls, what was I thinking, am I that dumb,

blind, trusting, that easy to fool, the customer with a hard-on and nothing else, just a play thing, a doll with

button eyes, shortsighted,

and stuffed.

We were clams, thought the young man while staring at Kim's body, she

let me believe I was something that I was not, that she was something that she wasn't, but in the end, right now, it's like we were both nothing the whole time, and worse, that we brought more nothing to each other, added to the nothingness inside of ourselves, and

after all I did, all I risked, and all for lies that started out being ideals, everything turned to mist and then evaporated,

all of it gone

in the right light.

We were clams, thought the young man while staring at Kim's body, she

was the poetry of Suchoon Mo, something blessed

and screwed up

all at the same time.

☙ THE TRACKS WERE ON FIRE

The tracks were on fire but the train kept rolling. The

tracks were on fire and it was enough to make a young pyromaniac cum his pants. The tracks were on fire while I

snorted vicodin in Vermont. The

tracks were on fire while I thought about France. The tracks were on fire and I

didn't have a name, or a face, or a body, or a soul, I was just
something dreamt up

by some
imbalanced kid
in a dark room. The tracks were on fire and the train kept rolling.
The tracks were

on fire and I was typing Dempsey-brand poetry

in my bedroom with the lights off. The tracks were on fire while
men shot at each other. The tracks were on fire and the world
was on a handcart

rolling
through it all. The tracks were on fire while the guy down the
block

thought of being sucked off by 2 virgins
with braces and pigtails. The tracks were on fire while addicts
waited for phone calls. The tracks were on fire while Castro
remembered that

trick with the dove. The tracks were on fire as painters put
brushes
to cathedral
ceilings. The tracks were on fire and the conductor just kept
laughing,

laughing,

laughing at us all.

○R I BOUGHT IT

Sometimes you'll try something on with
no intention of buying it. You'll see it in a shop window,
act on impulse, walk in, touch it
and your mind goes

ooh

at the texture. Then the next thing you know you're
in the dressing room. You slip off
something old, and slide into
something new, look yourself over in the mirror, admiring
how well
it fits, how the color
brings out your eyes, works with your skin tone, and screw the
high
price,

you walk out
with a shopping bag in your hand.

Like that whole
'I'm you!' bit that I've been playing with lately. One

look
in the mirror,

and I saw that it was cut

just right for me.

CR MY DIRTY MUSE

I was typing in bed. A story. Not a great story, but one that had
to come out. I was stuck on a line. 20 minutes.

20 minutes staring at 3 words and that's no good. Says the tank's
coming close to empty.

I looked around the room and saw I was alone. I had a feeling
she had run off when I wasn't looking.

Then I heard her through the window. She was cooing, making
baby noises, giggling.

I ran outside, followed the noises, looked over a fence, and there
she was, sitting Indian style, topless, in the neighbor's backyard,
tickling a 3-year-old boy who reached for her hair.

Unbelievable.

That's the same game she played with me when I was that age.

"Hey!"

"Oh. Hi Johnny!"

She waved at me with innocence, smiling, her tits swinging from side to side and the 3-year-old gurgling.

"What the hell are you doing over there?"

She got up and walked over, still smiling, her tattoos visible (across her chest, along her ribs, over her belly button), and moving with her steps, and there's lots of them, all of them the names of dead men that I refuse to mention here.

The 3-year-old started bawling when he realized she was leaving him.

I understood how he felt.

"I was just having some fun. And it's so dark in that room."

"I know honey, but we're supposed to be working. You know that."

"I was trying Johnny, but you kept losing focus. Every 5 minutes you have to take a piss, or get a beer, or crush up pills, or roll a cigarette. I don't like that."

She's almost like any other woman.

"I'm sorry baby, from now on you get me- 100 percent. Promise."

She hops over the fence and I see up her skirt. More tattoos. More names, (on her feet, shins, thighs) and none of them my name.

"You don't know what those tattoos do to me. All those names. All those guys. I have to admit, it makes me a little jealous sometimes."

"Well, I can keep my clothes on if you want, while we're working anyway."

"No, no honey. I want you comfortable."

"You just like looking at my body, you're a pervert."

"I'm just a tiny bit of pervert. But you really are something to look at."

"Oooh, you really think so Johnny?"

She likes compliments, undivided attention, and when she calls, I've gotta sit up, shake, roll over like any other house pet.

"You know I do baby. Now let's get back inside and finish up this story. We're almost done."

We get back in the room. Her clothes disappear.

"What were you doing to that little kid out there?"

"Johnny's jealous. Johnny's jealous."

"No I'm not."

"Don't worry. I was just toying with him."

"Promise?"

"Cross my heart. He'll grow up to be an office manager and write rhyming poetry till he's 50. You know you're the only one that I care about."

"Yeah, but that's how we got started together. Besides, it's a rotten trick to play on people, letting them get a peak and then pulling it away like that."

She doesn't answer at first. She looks off into space, reminiscing.

"It was so much fun watching you grow up. Remember all the dirty things I made you do in the shower?"

"Yeah, I remember honey."

"And all the trouble we used to cause in school together."

"Yeah, all that trouble. You got me suspended in the 5th grade."

"Yeah, and I also got you laid in the 6th so you shouldn't complain."

"I'm not complaining. You've always stuck by me, well, except for that one time."

"When?"

"Last year."

"You mean when you said those things to me?"

"But I had to say those things. You know that."

"You made me feel so cheap. You know how much it hurt?"

"I know honey, but I already apologized for it."

"Paychecks. Deadlines. Word counts. How could you say those things?"

"It was a slipup. It won't happen again. John's honor!"

"Pinky swear on it."

We lock fingers and she smiles. About 30 seconds ago she was ready to cry. She's almost like any other woman.

We get back to work. She whispers while my fingers move across the keyboard. The story gets finished, and it's a good story, better than I had expected. I light a cigarette for each of us.

We lay back against the mattress, both sweating a little, both a little out of breath.

"That was really something baby. We really hammered it that time."

"Yeah, that was good. It reminded me of when we were working on *Bailing Water*."

"Yup, I caught a glimpse of that myself, but didn't want to say anything."

"You know what Johnny?"

"What?"

"I've been thinking of getting another tattoo soon."

"Where at?"

And she turns over onto her stomach, more names (across shoulder blades, up and down her spine, covering her ass and the backs of both legs). She twists her arm around and points to a bare spot.

"You know how long I've left that spot empty for? Centuries. And you know why?"

"Why?"

"Because I was waiting for you. Another few years, no more than a decade, and it'll read Dempsey."

"Are you sure?"

She turns back over, looking sleepy.

"Positive. We're so close."

"I know honey. Almost there."

"Almost."

And we finish our cigarettes in silence.

I thought about my name on her back, it would look good there, surrounded by all those other guys.

And she thought of plans, plans she had made a

long

time ago.

ᴄᴫ Metrosexuals! Manhattan! The 21st Century!

I am currently typing this in a building that is situated in the epicenter of metrosexuality; the manicure, pedicure, waxing shops around here are bursting with squealing, young, limp-wristed types that are half a bottle of Shiraz away from some men's room confession:

"Ooh, he had glitter on his cheeks!" (after the first drink)

"His shirt was so colorful!" (refilling the glass)

"He wore the tightest striped pants I've ever seen!" (downing the wine)

"His shoes had to be Italian." (refill number two)

"He bought me a Cosmo and we sat by the window." (sipping thoughtfully)

"I wound up in his apartment with an apple in my mouth, my ankles rubbing against my ears... Boys,

I have seen the light!"

It's too much. The west village is filled with these guys. They crowd the streets in 80-dollar t-shirts (designer), 150-dollar jeans (pre-faded), they wear flip flops made by Versace, Kenneth Cole, Armani Exchange- yes, it's obviously a middle ground, a state of limbo for the sexually disoriented, but even more than that, I'd say it's a blast-off point, a launch pad for a rocket with a trajectory that will inevitably bring them to the heights of their stickiest

of sailor

below decks

dreams...You just can't respect them. Or at least I can't. (Damned fence straddlers! Literally!)

They don't have the guts to go out as full-fledged fags, and they're too scared of the dark to hang around in closets. It's too much.

It makes you long for the good old days when things were a bit more cut and dry. When you could look at someone, maybe talk to them for a few minutes, and know right off the bat whether or not there's a pair of kneepads in their back pocket... Now it's a guessing game:

"Just because I have more products in my medicine cabinet than your last two girlfriends combined does that necessarily mean that I'm gay?"

"Just because I listen to techno while I shower, and dance with women that I never seem to take home, does that make me queer?"

I say yes, and damned near full-blown.

In my opinion, metrosexuality is to homosexuality what the airport runway is to the sky. All these kids you see on the street are merely in training; they're building up their speed, checking their flaps (think about that and get disgusted), yelling "Roger! Roger!" into some stranger's ear, giggling while greasing their joints and gearboxes, checking the direction of the wind one last time ('Is it acceptable or not?' 'Will I be ostracized like a leper or received as a hero?') and preparing for some grand lift-off…Now,

as to the women who supposedly enjoy this behavior, who are attracted to the men they meet in their local hair salons, that smile at the guy in the shampoo aisle that reaches for the same bottle as they do, I can only think of two possibilities.

They are either fag hags (girls that absolutely need a man in their lives without the fear of getting drunk and waking up next to him naked and colored in body paint (they're missing out! Body paint can be fun, and if it's edible, even more so!)), or repressed lesbians that will take the most feminine man they can get their hands on. Someone who actually has the equipment to convince their girl friends that they really are straight and that it's ok for them to change together in the same dressing room (who's looking!), without worrying about blowjobs, morning erections, or demon whiskey dick pounding away at them at 3 o'clock in the morning…It's one, big, chaotic and confused mess of square pegs being forced into

round holes (a damned sexual conundrum!),

and hand-me-downs going from older sister to younger brother, and hand-me-ups working vice-versa…

"Larry, have you seen my eyelash curler?"

"Ooh, I think it's on my dresser."

"I don't mind if you use it, just try and put it back when you're done- ok?"

"Sorry sis, I completely forgot. I meant to put it back, but then Rico called and he had just finished watching *Bridget Jones' Diary*, and you know how much he likes Renee Zellweger."

"I loved that movie."

"Me too."

"Hey, Larry?"

"Yeah?"

"I'm going to the beach today, do you think I can borrow your sarong?"

"Which one?"

"The blue one, with the flowers and birds on it."

And Larry most probably has 5 sarongs hanging in his immaculate and organized closet, also mom's sweater- that looks so much better on him then it does on her- maybe a few pictures of Rico sitting in the park with his shirt off and sipping at an iced latte... This is the 21st century!

This is what I see and hear on the streets of Manhattan most every day of the week.

I walk around like a caveman. A relic of a time when if you had a dick you didn't wax your chest, put highlights in your hair, take 2 and a half hours to get dressed with your buddies and play grab-ass in front of the mirror.

Hell, growing up, if you were caught singing a Madonna song the kids in the neighborhood would beat hell out of you when they saw you on the street. Now, I'm sure that could be considered a little extreme, or irrational, but I think that I'd rather be an extreme and irrational person, than a minority in a world of ambiguous sexual identity.

  - John

✿ MOVIES? JOHN? IT COULD HAPPEN.

So I met with the Director last night. I left the job early, took a valium, smoked a roach on the 6 block walk to The Slaughtered Lamb (A little nervous John? Always!), positioned myself at the bar so I could watch the door in the reflection of the beer taps, ordered,

"Shot of Dewar's and a Bud."

I did that three times. I was ordering a fourth when the door swung open.

"John?"

"How's it going?"

The Director. She's done some film work, commercials, music videos, blessed with an eye for photography, understands the importance of cross angles in scenery, has won awards, hell, she even has a production company. (How do I know all this? I did my research, read her resume, watched clips of her short films, took a long look at her pictures; and I was fucking impressed!)

We start talking. What she's looking for: A writer to work with. Someone to produce a script, and not for a quickie film, but for a full-length feature- 90 minutes! She wants something dynamic, something real, something she can feel confident investing herself in. I tell her I've never written a script before. That I've only enjoyed 8 out of the last 100 movies I've watched. That I'm an egomaniac. That I have trouble writing about anyone or anything besides myself. She says,

"If I was doing a short film I would use any one of the stories that you sent me. (My submission pieces: Chicago, The Fight at the Bank, That Kid on Pulaski.) But what I need is something longer, at least 90 pages. And I want strong characters, strong dialogue, a decent plot without any unnecessary violence. I want something as good as your submissions, but longer."

I order that fourth round. Stare off into space for a few minutes. Think about her legs because she was wearing one hell of a nice skirt that kept inching and riding up her thighs and she was crossing, re-crossing, her legs, Dewar's and valium and dreaming about her panties- Relax John. Be a professional. This is an opportunity here. The cosmos conspiring so that the light of some third sun on some distant planet can reach the earth…

"I already have a director of photography on board. We've raised enough money to start production work. Now we need a script."

"O.k."

"I like your writing John. My boyfriend ordered both of your books after he read your submission. And to be honest with you, I think you would be perfect for something like this."

I was thinking how I should've taken 2 valiums instead of 1. The place is air-conditioned. I'm wearing a short-sleeved shirt. I've got enough liquor in me to slow my heart rate, to make my blood sluggish, yet I was sweating- John! You taffy ass! You fairy! John you're a fucking pixie or sprite or something. You're a little girl having her hymen broken and feeling embarrassed about the blood!

"Hey, you mind if I step outside to smoke a cigarette?"

I stood on the corner and contemplated running away. I was thinking how my book bag was still inside, but how I could always come back for it tomorrow.

Then I thought about her legs again, what they would look like while she was running. I started giggling to myself. I remembered how just last week I started a fight with 6 muscle-bound football players at the beach. They had accidentally clipped The Blonde's chair with bad passes- twice, and that was enough for me to react.

They were big, tattooed, one kid had his front tooth missing…I had a bottle in my hand though. I was also smart enough to stand by a metal garbage can so I could crack the thing if it was needed. I said a few things. The kind of things you'd hear in an alley, in a prison yard, the kind of things that would either enrage someone with a temper, or force urine down the legs of the spineless.

They kept looking back and forth between my eyes and the bottle, saw that things would escalate, get ugly…eventually, they backed down. They apologized, walked away. They could've whipped my ass up and down that beach, but I had somehow scared them off…John Dempsey! Guardian of The Blonde! And here I was, a little baby rabbit afraid of failure…I tossed the cigarette, went back inside, and ordered a fifth round.

"Director."

"Yeah?"

"Give me a week to get some ideas together."

After she left I stayed in the bar for a while. Then I got on the subway, then on the train, I was fidgeting in the seat and drinking 16-ounce cans of Budweiser, staring out the window (Do you really think you can do it John? I have no idea man. I don't know if I'm ready or not for something like this, but I have to give it a shot. I agree, this is one of the greatest opportunities ever presented to you- fucking run with it! Invest yourself in it! Bleed for this thing or you'll curse your yellow face in the mirror every morning!).

I watched the buildings and the people whip by, thought about fate, the future, thought about the possibilities… I fell asleep and woke up 2 hours later in the train yard. I got out, found a payphone, and made a collect call to The Blonde.

She picked me up about 40 minutes later, took one look at me,

"I'm not even going to ask. You'll tell me when you're ready. But I know something happened to you today."

And I guess something did happen. I'm still not sure how to feel about any of it. I'm letting the back brain work it out for now. I'm figuring that soon something will explode, a special synapse will fire, some literary match will flare up under my ass and I'll be forced to run to the machine…I wonder how all this will turn out.

ℭℛ MOVIES? JOHN? IT COULD HAPPEN – PART 2

I'm doing it! The Director gave me the green light last week. I pitched her a story that blew up in my head bigger, brighter, louder than a 15-inch mortar exploding in a broom closet…I typed out a 5 page synopsis, she thought about it for a week or so, spoke with some of the people involved with the project, met me in a dive bar in the East Village, said John,

"I want this story. It's so dark and at the same time so pretty."

Ha-ha! (so pretty!) I giggle hard enough to shake the stool, laugh loud enough to wake sleeping drunks, tell her I need to step outside for a cigarette…It takes 7 minutes for me to calm down. I walk back in the place,

"Director, before we get started on anything I've gotta ask you three questions."

"O.k."

"First, are you behind this thing one hundred percent? You need to understand that if I start on this, I'm going to see it through till the end. I'm going to have to do some fucked up things to get it down. I need to know that you're committed to this as much as I am."

"Without a question. I want this story. I can direct this thing. I'm already seeing how to shoot it."

"Alright, next, let's say I get this script together the way it should be. All the i's dotted, all the movement, everything as wild and vivid as I see it in my head…then I want to watch it happen. I want to see it all in action, from picking of locations to casting, editing the whole bit. I won't jump up and criticize, I won't be a pain in the ass or get in the way, I just want to see it. I want to be there, watching it come together. Is that possible?"

"Not a problem. I want you there. You know this story better than anyone else. I'd say I need you there."

"Awesome, so far so good, last question, and I'm being serious here, Director, every time you've met me I've been on my best behavior. I've controlled myself, been an upstanding young man and all, but you need to know it won't always be like this. You're getting a side of John that my parent's rarely see. I'm sure there will be times when I wind up getting a little out of hand, just a bit crazy, but I won't do anything to fuck with this project, do you think you can handle that?"

"Ha! I was waiting for you to stop being so damned nice. I've read enough of your work to know how you are, or at least get an idea of it. Yes, I think I can handle it."

I stuck out my hand,

"Okay Director, let's make a movie."

I did a lot of thinking over the weekend. Took a few pills and let my brain work everything out. Had a few dreams filled with signs, omens. Curled up behind The Blonde and kissed at her neck, back, lips for hours…everything pointing in the same direction, I slid myself in as the sun came through my window, heart rate doubled, the moan of justified anticipation…I actually think I may be ready.

THE DEMPSEY INSTITUTE OF LITERATURE

1

Many writers either have, or have had, a problem with drugs and alcohol. It's a fact. And because of this fact many people who want to be writers turn to drugs and alcohol in order to kick start the creative process. But that's all wrong. The only thing needed to write is a pulse. You can't write unless you're alive and maybe that's where the drugs and alcohol come in. Me, for example, I haven't been sober more than 4 hours in the last 10 years. I fall into bed dead drunk each night, wake up with my head buzzing, chew painkillers, get in the shower, and by the time I step out of the shower the day has become something soft and manageable. I can breathe. I have a pulse and it's a strong pulse and it's the only thing needed. That pulse lets me write. It lets me dream and think outside of myself, it lets me travel, blast off the earth and go shooting through space for a while. Maybe that's a weakness. Maybe it's escapist mentality. But I don't quite give a shit. If I wasn't in a constant state of sedation I'd be loony. I'd set banks on fire, slap around my girlfriend, piss in mailboxes or cut myself with razors. I know it doesn't sound right, but all that intake helps me to stay out of jail cells and sanitariums. Sure, maybe in the long run I'll wind up on the street, or who knows, maybe a rehab in Florida, but still, as long as I've put down enough words before any of that happens it'll be worth it. I'll at least be able to say that I once had a pulse, and that I used that pulse to dream, to move, to write.

2

A few months ago I sat in bed for close to a week, drinking beer and chewing pills nonstop. I barely slept. I didn't eat. I couldn't fuck. All I did was intake, intake, intake- fantastic! Empty cans lined the headboard of my bed, all my bookshelves and they almost looked like sports trophies. My bank account was empty and all the money that had been in it was split between the cash register at the beer disburser, and the wallet of my pill connection. I drew on my stomach with markers, and every time I doubted myself, or thought about what I was doing, I said 5 words out loud, 'Think only of your art.' It kept away the depression. It stopped all the second guessing. I knew that I was simply working on maintaining my pulse, staying alive in order to get back at the machine once the tanks had been filled up.

3

That's part of the creative process. You have to get yourself to the point where you are alive- mentally- and then your fingers go to autopilot, and the words move like speeding trains or exotic birds or Russian ballerinas. Sure. Your keystrokes become the brushstrokes of Jim Dine, the earth rotates around your work, and every orgasm on the planet ends in someone screaming your name. That's how it gets after a while. That's what a pulse does. That's what happens when you're alive, and so you work on staying that way so that the brushstrokes, rotations and orgasms never end. You know that once the canvas remains empty, once the world stops turning, once the jizz stops spurting, you know that you're screwed- and that simply can't happen. You cannot allow that to happen. Just look at Ernie. Talk about losing the pulse. Poor fucking guy, he threw it all to the bulls and stopped breathing.

4

So what you need to do is figure out how to keep up that pulse, how to stay alive. After that comes the laughter and the dancing girls. After that is euphoria. The real drugs are your words. You snort your sentences and go buzzing off towards sunrise. You drink your stories by the bottle, and if you overdo it, wake up with a hangover and gag into the toilet, then you'll know it's a good story and that it was as intoxicating as absinthe.

5

The Dempsey Institute of Literature! Sure! There's only one professor (me), only one course (how to stay alive), and it's pass or fail, sink or swim, type or throw yourself from the roof of the highest building you can find. I won't even charge tuition. But if you feel like donating a little something it'll be appreciated. Come to class with a 12-pack and offer me a couple of bottles. Get someone to write you a prescription for oxycontin and drop a hundred milligrams or so onto my desk. Wear a mini-skirt and sit in the front row, crossing, and uncrossing your legs. I'm not greedy, I don't want it all. Hell, just a taste, just a fix, you can even wear panties and I wouldn't mind. Just give what you can, of what you have, and all the knowledge rattling around my chemically addled brains will be imparted to you, my dear student.

6

Okay. Has everyone brought their pulse with them to class today? Raise your hands if you haven't and you can be excused from today's lecture. And don't try lying to me because I've got a stethoscope in my drawer- anyone even suspected of showing up here dead will be examined, and if I don't hear that thump in your chest then you'll be asked to leave. It's that simple. I'm not much for rules, but I refuse to have zombies in my classroom. I want you breathing. I want you bursting with life. I will only train comets and ripe tomatoes. All you black holes and old fruits will not get anything out of this. You'll just waste my time and space and I simply won't allow that. That's my job. Alright, today we're going to talk about experience. It's almost as important as a pulse and without it all your words are counterfeit. It will be obvious that they are counterfeit. The truth of the matter is that you just can't write what you don't know. You have to have experience. If you want to write about heroin then you've got to have a habit. If you want to write about being in the gutter then you've got to have spent some time sleeping on the street. If you want to write about whores, then I better have seen you, at least once, pacing in front of that free clinic in Hempstead, hoping that no one you know will drive by and recognize you. Now, if you want to write about unicorns, talking frogs, or goats that grant wishes, well, then you may as well get the fuck out of here right now. This isn't the place for that. I'm not saying that you can't use your imagination- I do it all the time- but without truth behind your words, without knowledge of exactly what it is, how it tastes, what it feels, smells, looks like, how it reacts when you kiss its neck, how it squeals with 3 fingers in it, then you may as well apply for a job at Hallmark.

7

Experience! Truth! If you write without these things then you're as obvious as a virgin fumbling with hooks and rolling the condom on backwards. I'm not telling you to pick up a needle, or live in a cardboard box. I'm not telling you to call an escort service (regardless of how much fun it may be to spend your paycheck on your back). What I'm saying is that you will not find the right words, the real words that are needed to give life to a piece of paper, until you've lived what it is that you want to type. It just won't work. For instance, I once tried writing a long story about cowboys that hung out on a ranch called the KY

Corral. I got 15 pages in and realized it was garbage. It was all false. Why? Because I don't know anything about cowboys. I've never hung out with a cowboy. I've never even talked to cowboy. Sure, I know about KY, but that isn't enough. It's nowhere near enough. Now, if I had spent time in the Midwest, riding horses and goosing cowhands, then maybe I would've been able to write that kind of a story. That story taught me a lesson, and now I'm turning that lesson over to you. Don't write what you don't know. It's fraud. You're cheating yourself and whatever unlucky asshole gets stuck reading you. It's the same as going out with some knockout girl, getting her drunk, slipping your hand up her shirt and coming away with tissue paper. It's like falling in love with some post-op transvestite, and then after months of dating she tells you that her birth certificate reads Tom, or Charley, or Kevin or something. Think about how you would feel. She says, 'Here's a picture of what I used to look like.' And it's some dude with buckteeth and an 8-inch cock.

8

Let's keep it moving. Another thing that you'll need is discipline. I wake up in the morning, and think about how nice it would be to just lay in bed all day jerking off. I don't want to think. I don't want to talk, move, nothing. I just want to stay warm under the covers creating stains. How nice does that sound? What a life that would be! There's no rejection, no effort involved, a party of one and you get to be both the host and the guest of honor. Talk about perfection! But it can't be done. Sure, here and there you can take some time for yourself. You can rent dirty movies and give your forearms a workout. There's nothing wrong with that. But masturbation will only take you so far. You've got to roll into the morning and get in front of that machine no matter how tired, hung over, sad, you may feel. You've got to come to terms with the fact that the only way to get through life is typing your way out. If you want to write, there just isn't any other way. There's no backdoor, no shortcuts, no write by the numbers bullshit that will make you great. Let's talk about Dr. Frankenstein; do you think he brought his creation to life by spitting in his palm and sticking 2 fingers in his ass? Of course not! He worked. He worked hard. He didn't go out to nightclubs or movie theaters twice a week. He locked himself in his laboratory and experimented until he found the right way to bring life to something that anyone else would've left dead. Be like Frankenstein! Be Prometheus! Bust your ass until you can take from the gods what they have been hoarding for so long- and then when you have it, make it yours. That's next.

9

Originality! Everybody knows what Bukowski reads like. Everybody knows what Thompson, Kozinski, Celine, Miller, Fante, Dostoevsky, Hemingway, Faulkner, Dos Passos, Burroughs, Fitzgerald, Conrad, Saroyan, Burgess, Ginsberg, etc. read like. If you plan on imitating your heroes, then you may as well be a Xerox machine. Learn from them, look up to them, sure, there's nothing wrong with that. But the first time you try copying them I will kick your Xerox machine ass right out of the room and tell you never to show your carbon paper shit face around here again. I'm serious. That isn't writing. It's actually the farthest thing from writing and you may as well become a police officer or a financial analyst or something. I don't mean to be harsh, but you've got to understand that all those guys you see sitting on the shelves in the bookstore have been read, categorized and memorized by a million different dreamers. Those same dreamers are your audience. Those are the ones you want hanging on your words, buying your books, going to your website, sending you letters telling you that they think about you at night and it forces them to bite pillows. That should be your goal. Define yourself in terms of yourself. Every time I type something I read it over 5, 6, sometimes 20 different times to make sure that it resembles one thing and one thing only- Dempsey! I pound away at my keyboard, doing and giving everything that is in me in an attempt to create something that has never before been read, ingested, or smuggled through customs in the lower intestines of a mule. Create- Create- Create! Anything else is a lie. Anything else is empty. Anything else is a one-way ticket to the void of normality and you will never be able to distinguish yourself from all the other bullshit bootleggers in the world.

10

And that's all there is to it. Besides luck anyway. But that's something that you can't do anything about and so you may as well not think about it. Leave that to the guys picking lotto numbers. There are a few other things, but I think you've had enough. Right now, what you need to do is sit down and write. Write until you move yourself. Write until your fingers get sore, until you become hooked on your own words, until you feel real and brilliant and luminous. Write until you become the sun, until you're the atom bomb, until you're a god! Write until you catch a glimpse of yourself on the page and it feels so good, so right, it feels as if all of heaven was in your lap and you were being sucked off by angels. Write your own personal world into existence. Write space and beyond. Just write.

Disclaimer: Do not listen to any of the things I've just told you. If you haven't figured it out by now, I'm an idiot and a degenerate and anyone who takes me seriously should be locked up in a psyche ward. (I'm also a sexual deviant who doesn't know what day it is, gets confused by his own reflection in the mirror, that can't be trusted to write travel brochures let alone literature. I'm also an egomaniac with a schizoid personality, and everything I've ever written reeks of everything I've ever read. I'm more monster than Frankenstein, and all you townspeople should be chasing me with flaming torches! You should be buying handguns and stilettos in anticipation of seeing me on the street! You should buy my books and use them like they were expensive kindling! Sure.) But if, under some strange set of circumstances, you do take me seriously, and you have managed to keep clear of the loony bin, and you would like further instruction, well, then send me an email with your name, a sample of your work, a picture of yourself with one of my poems tucked between your legs, and you'll be considered for enrollment.

   - John.

෬ I COULD'VE BEEN

a million different things, you name it

and I'd find a way to pull it off, I'd

make it magical and dynamic- no question about it!-

but

it would've all been a lie, it would've all lead to homemade
gallows, so instead

I'm just john,

the typist, the escape artist, the pervert, the malcontent, the one

behind all these keystrokes

making those old

Asians

clap (applause, and Bravo!, as I exit stage left,

and off

the page)

www.ingramcontent.com/pod-product-compliance
Lightning Source LLC
Chambersburg PA
CBHW072057170626
46813CB00004B/1397